Hotwife In Victorian England - A Victorian England Wife Watching Romance Novel

Karly Violet

Published by Karly Violet, 2023.

This is a work of fiction. Similarities to real people, places, or events are entirely coincidental.

HOTWIFE IN VICTORIAN ENGLAND - A VICTORIAN ENGLAND WIFE WATCHING ROMANCE NOVEL

First edition. August 28, 2023.

ISBN: 979-8223253570

Written by Karly Violet.

Hotwife In Victorian England

A Victorian England Wife Watching Romance Novel

Individuals on the cover are models and are used for illustrative purposes only.

Author's note: All character in this story are 18 years of age and older.

This is a work of fiction, any resemblance to real live name or events are purely coincidental.

Be aware: This story is written for, and should only be enjoyed by, ADULTS. It includes explicit descriptions of intense sexual activity between consenting adults.

Note that this work of fiction resembles a fantasy world, all events taking place aré a result of a role play amongst all parties and all parties are fully consenting adults.

Hotwife First Time

Chapter One: The Law be Damned

I'm a gentleman of high birth. My father, the great Henry Hutchins, would die again if he knew that I represent a man of Mr. Rupert Crowley's standing. At eighty-one years of age, it's quite the accomplishment for the street beggar to have survived so long. Perhaps it has a great deal to do with the old man's capacity to evoke sympathy from those who pass him in the street. Then again, his manners are often ill-presented when he crosses those of greater standing than he.

"Well, Mr. Hutchins? Will this scoundrel pay the ten shillings he owes the court?" Judge Edward Downs peers at us from beneath his powdered wig.

"My lord," I begin as I look nervously from my client to him. "Mr. Crowley would like to petition your honour for another two weeks."

"It has already been three, sir," the judge answers with a scowl on his face. "Should I raise the fine to double?"

The old beggar beside me narrows his eyes and begins to speak before I can stop him. "You might as well hit me with a pound. I have it as much as I have a single farthing to my name."

"Hush," I say under my breath to Mr. Crowley.

"How dare you address this court in such a way!" The judge looks down at the small man. "It would behoove you to remember who I am lest I should assign you to the whip as well!"

"Your Honour," I plead with him. "My client is four scores and a year. He would not survive any lashing upon his feeble person."

"Then silence that fool," Judge Downs bellows back at me. It's remarkable how loudly such a small man can transmit his voice when angry with someone like the man beside me. The judge isn't well known for being patient or compassionate, no matter the person before him.

"He will not speak out of turn again," I promise as I look at Mr. Crowley sternly. I can tell that my client would like to say something else, but even he appears to come to the understanding that he is close to having the skin torn from his back.

"Another two weeks is unacceptable," the judge says after a moment's thought. "I will increase the fine by five shillings and require payment by the first of the month, Mr. Hutchins. Will that be agreeable, or should I put this poor soul to the lash?" His dark eyes pierce me as Judge Downs stares at me. I nod my head, realizing that the one week and a day that Mr. Crowley has been given is much better than the beating at the end of a whip. However, another five shillings have been added to the cost and will need to be paid or he will find himself incarcerated for at least a month in the Southampton jail.

"Thank you, my lord. He will pay."

"Agreed. One way or another." The judge brings down his gavel before rising to his feet along with the others in the courtroom. He walks out and then I turn to look at Mr. Crowley.

"Can you pay anything?" I ask.

"I did nothing," he complains. "She wouldn't move and so she got what she got." His weathered face turns into a scowl as he shakes his head. "Damned dame."

"You know you should not have spat in her way," I retort. "She is a lady, not some common wash woman, Mr. Crowley. There are laws to be considered."

"Damn the laws," he spits as we walk out of the courtroom. "Damn that insufferable judge."

I take the old man by the arm and pull him close. "You should bite your tongue, Mr. Crowley. We are still within earshot of those who might report to his Honour."

"His *Honour?"* he laughs. "I should have spat upon the floor while in the courtroom. That would have shown him my thoughts better, aye?"

"Mr. Crowley." I look hard at him. "Do you have any money at all?"

He narrows his eyes. "Do I look like a banker to you, young master? Of course I have nothing. Not one penny."

I sigh. "You'll die in that jail," I warn him. "Can you get it within the week?"

Mr. Crowley shakes his head. "I'm not of a mind to pay. No, I think I'll look that wigged bastard in the eyes and tell him to bloody well rock off!"

"You damned old fool," I mumble as I shake my head. "Keep the clothes," I tell him. "And the shoes. The undertaker had spares and he doesn't want them back." I lie. The mortuary man did want the clothes back, borrowed quickly when I noticed that Mr. Crowley was barely wearing anything when he arrived outside the courthouse. The judge would certainly have put him in jail if he had shown up in such a sorry state of dress. Unfortunately, there is little forgiveness in polite society for the likes of Rupert Crowley.

"Fine things to wear. See, young master, things are already much better." Mr. Crowly smiles and makes his way to the front doors. As he leaves, I wonder whether he'll attempt to mend his ways when it comes to the way he treats those above his station. Somehow, I doubt it.

"I'm going to pay the fine for Mr. Crowley," I tell the court clerk when I arrive at his office next to the courtroom.

He eyes me and shakes his head. "Another charity case, Mr. Hutchins?"

I chuckle. "It's fifteen shillings now and Mr. Crowley has naught. I couldn't get the judge to lower the fine."

"Fifteen shillings, eh? What did he do?"

I shake my head. "Spat upon the path of a young lady."

The clerk frowns. "It's a heavy fine for such a thing, even for that wretch."

"She is the niece of the local land commissioner," I reply. "She's well connected and very easily offended by spittle."

"I see." He makes out the payment note as I pull the shillings from my pocket. I lay them out on the desk before the clerk and take the note into my pocket. At least Rupert Crowley will not be going into Southampton jail anytime soon.

"Thank you, sir." I nod my head and the clerk returns the same before I turn and walk out of his office. Making my way out of the courthouse, I begin to think about the others I have represented before the judge over the last few weeks. It seems as if I am losing many more cases than I am winning. My wife will be none too pleased that I've essentially paid the way of yet another poor lowlife.

"I am sorry, Father. I know that you would be so disappointed in the solicitor I have become, but I cannot allow Mr. Crowley or any other dredge of society to pay for their unfortunate circumstances when the cost is so high." I've always felt that the lower rungs of our society are forgotten and uncared for in a way that is quite shameful. The good church people of Southampton do what they can for Mr. Crowley and his ilk, but there are often too many to keep from harm.

"Kind sir," I hear a voice say from behind me. A woman, dirty and smelling of horse dung, approaches me. "Thank you for the bread."

"Bread?" I don't know what she's talking about until I recall something from the other day. "Samuel?"

"Aye, Sammy," she says with a smile. "You gave him bread when he came by your office last week. It fed us for two days." She reaches for me and takes my hand, the dirt upon it gritting against my palm. Though I feel a bit repulsed, I do not pull away immediately. "We thank you for your kindness, dear sir."

I nod my head. "He seemed to need it more than I."

"Aye, sir. We did." She pulls her hands from me. Something about her tells me that the woman is looking for something more. I look past her and see her son sitting next to a carriage nearby. He is the reason she knows my identity this morning.

I reach into my pocket and pull out two shillings. It is all that I have left after paying Mr. Crowley's fine. "It's enough to eat. Go and be full," I tell her.

"So kind!" She reaches her arms around me, the odor of her body almost overwhelming me as the woman squeezes me tightly.

"Bless you both," I reply. She backs away and turns toward her son. As she gets back to him, he gets up and they walk away together. I know they have likely been scheming to find a way to get more from me. It's an unfortunate way of life in Southampton for those of lesser standing. Once they have discovered that someone will help, they continue to squeeze them until their benefactors drip no more.

I turn and continue walking home. The day has been long and I look forward to seeing my Emma soon. Her beautiful green eyes sooth my soul when I am troubled and today I am quite troubled. Tomorrow will bring more afflictions, of this I am certain. However, I live for today. What comes tomorrow will only matter when the sun once again rises in the east.

Chapter Two: Incredible Beauty

I walk into the house before handing over my coat and valise to our butler, Carlton. He quietly takes my things and turns to put them away as I make my way toward the dining room. I find Emma waiting for me at the doorway with a smile on her face.

"Hello, dear husband," she says with a slight Irish accent before we trade kisses on the cheeks. Emma has been trying to learn a more English accent so as to draw less attention to herself when we attend galas together. Some in polite society are not as *polite* as they should be.

"Hello, dear wife." I smile at my beautiful Emma, her light brown hair neatly put up in a tight bun atop her head. Her green eyes look softly into mine as she takes my hand and leads me into the dining room. This has been our tradition for nearly six years since offering our vows to one another.

As we take our places at the table, a footman pushes in Emma's chair. I sit down and wait patiently as a plate of food is served to her before I am given an identical fare. Wine is then poured for the two of us and we begin our evening culinary experience.

"Very nice," Emma says as she finishes her first bite of cheese and bread. She turns to her soup, the sort of meal she would have enjoyed in Dublin before moving to Southampton to marry me.

"A fine day for you today, my love?" I ask as I smile at her.

She nods her head. "A fine day indeed." Her Irish dialect becomes slightly thicker as she speaks to me. Emma often allows herself to become more at ease around me. I adore this about her. "I took the liberty of walking to the butcher and asking for a bit of bacon."

I raise an eyebrow. "*You* went to the butcher? My love, we have a cook to make that journey. Surely you didn't need to make an appearance there." Many in our social circles would scoff at the idea of darkening the doorstep of any butcher, baker, or cobbler. No, we have servants for such things.

"You know that I like to see where from what we eat comes." Her accent is now as thick as I've ever known it. Emma has a ways to go before erasing her upbrought way of speaking.

"The cook is perfectly capable," I assure her. "Give her the task next time, Emma. She will always choose the finest." I put a bite of bread into my mouth as I stare at my wife. "You are perfectly beautiful, my love. Perfectly beautiful."

Her face turns a little pink before my wife changes the subject. "How was your day, James? Weren't you to be in court this morn'?"

I nod my head. "Yes, I was in court today for most of the day. I was involved in three cases in particular."

Emma smiles. "And what about that one street man? What was his name again?" Her green eyes softly gaze in my direction as she takes a break from eating her meal. We sometimes talk about the specifics of our days, and it's true that I have told her about the old man I represented before the judge.

"Rupert Crowley," I answer before putting a bite of cheese into my mouth and chewing.

"Rupert." Emma nods her head. "Did the judge toss him into a cage? I'd wager he had nothing to give."

I swallow hard. "The judge gave him another few days and increased the penalty to fifteen shillings. It all worked out, though. Mr. Crowley is now free of his burden to the court." Reaching for my glass of wine, I pick it up and put it to my lips. The sip of wine is both sweet and bitter, likely because I know what's coming.

Emma narrows her eyes. "James, you didn't pay the man's fine for him, did you?" I don't answer, but that's as good as a clear affirmation for my Irish bride. "We've spoken of this before, my love. You should not give out charity to criminals."

"He spat in front of a woman. I don't see how it's fair to levy a fine so high when he would have been fined five shillings or less for striking another of his kind."

She shakes her head. "Your duty as solicitor is to represent the poor devils like him, James. Not to pay their fines!" Emma shakes her head as she looks hard at me. "My father became what he became because he didn't give it all away."

"We're already quite wealthy," I remind her. "We don't need the money from those such as Mr. Crowley anyway."

"But you're a *solicitor,*" Emma chides. "Your father was a solicitor of the highest sort and he expected much more of you." My wife is from Dublin, her father a wealthy coal supplier. She understands wealth very well, but at times she doesn't quite have a solid understanding of the compassion I feel for those like Rupert Crowley.

"I didn't ask to be a solicitor," I answer her. "My father demanded that I follow him into this, but it wasn't my life's true concern."

"It is your concern now," Emma tells me. "You are a solicitor whether you would have chosen it or not. Your father, Heaven rest him, was concerned about you and your future. Give heed, husband, to your upbringing and your calling."

I sigh. "My *calling* is to be generous and kind to my fellow man, Emma. My *profession* is that of a solicitor."

Emma shakes her head. She knows me all too well. I'm not the sort to easily back away from my firmest convictions. Smiling, my wife says to me, "I married you because of your soft heart and warm soul, James." Her green eyes turn back to her meal and she begins to eat once again. My mind begins to wander as I think about what my father expected of me.

"You are to be a man of highest integrity, Jimmy." These words still ring loudly in my ears. *"Stand before the court and make your case. Be honorable. The law is the law and there is nothing else. Men are simply animals without the law to make the bounds."*

"Is the soup too cool?" I look up to see a footman standing near the table. I've held my spoon over the small bowl for a bit too long and he has begun to wonder about the condition of the brothy water.

I shake my head. "No. It's perfectly fine." I nod my head and watch him step back into his place. Though it's good to have the wealth to do as Emma and I see fit, it sometimes bothers me to know that there are others standing nearby who will jump up and come to our service for such small things. Perhaps if I had been brought up in a lower station in life I would have been happier, but I would never trade for such. After all, it's because of my place in society that I happened to meet my lovely wife.

"You should consider working at the soup kitchen if you wish to help those less fortunate," Emma tells me as she attempts to clear the thick accent from her words once again. "The ladies and I have been doing that for the last year or two."

"Maybe," I reply with a smile. "But then again, I have little interest in that as opposed to what I'm already doing." I take a sip of wine. "My love, you are as charitable as I."

Emma laughs. "Charitable? I only pour the soup. It's hardly charity, James."

"It's charity," I tell her. "And a good thing for honest upstanding people to do."

"Charity." Emma raises an eyebrow. "Fine. Charity it is, then." She shakes her head and smiles as she lifts her wine glass to her lips. She then nods toward the footman. "I have some letters to write to home, my love, if that's agreeable."

"Very much, my dear." I stand to my feet as the footman pulls the chair back for Emma. I watch as she leaves the dining room before I sit back down. The footman then turns and walks over to my end of the table.

"Have a seat, Rodney," I tell the young man as I smile. He pulls a chair out and has a seat nearby. It's the sort of thing that we do when my wife leaves the dining room, as she almost always does before I do.

"Thank you, sir," he replies. "May I speak freely?" I nod my head. "You are an honorable gentleman, sir," Rodney begins. "What you did for that poor street dweller is a good thing. A very good thing."

I look over at the footman and smile. "I'm glad that you think so, Rodney. I couldn't simply let him go to that filthy dungeon they call a jail."

He smiles. "I know that many of those you represent to the court are not very thankful for what you do for them, but it is well thought of by your house staff, sir. We are all proud to serve you and your wife." Rodney bows his head a little and I smile.

"You and the others here are like family." Of course, Rodney would have never dared to have taken a seat next to me at the table if Emma was still present in the room. No, she expects the help to be succinctly professional in nature. Mixing work with pleasantries isn't the sort of thing that she allows. It's fun to have this little secret with Rodney and the other household staff.

"If you should ever need anything, please let us know. We are pleased to be at your service." He again bows his head before getting up from his chair. Rodney moves toward the other end of the table where he picks up my wife's plates and wine glass before walking out of the dining room. The silence in the room causes me to think again about my father and his expectations of me.

"Never allow a good case to pass you by, Jimmy." My father would often refer to me as Jimmy whenever he spoke to me. At least, until I became a full member of the bar. Once that happened, he began to refer to me as James Hutchins, partner. Hutchins & Hutchins has become a powerful law firm in its own right because of the work my father put into it. However, if he knew now that I was taking on such cases as those of Rupert Crowley, he might be less than enthused to refer to me as partner. No, I believe he would be very unhappy with me.

"Be prepared to keep their secrets, my boy. Those of high station in this life oft have less savory skeletons in their proverbial closets. It is upon you to keep those skeletons hidden. Buried, if you will."

I swallow hard as the hair stands up along the back of my neck. There are occasions when I feel as if the elder Mr. Hutchins is watching me from just behind. Maybe he is. Maybe he disapproves of my decisions when it comes to those of lesser birth. It doesn't really matter, though. The firm is now mine to do with as I please. If I wish to defend those less fortunate, I will. I cannot unmake the sort of man that I am. Nor do I desire to do so. If my father cannot be proud of me for that, so what?

I get up from my seat just as Rodney returns. He scoops up my plates and glass as I turn and walk toward the dining room door. A last look of approval comes from the footman as we part company. My heart beats a little more powerfully as I think about the good I have done today. I can be proud of that, if not for the earnings in the firm's coffers. Emma and I have been truly blessed with our standing in this life. It hurts no one to spread that out a little to our fellow men.

Chapter Three: Not Up to Dick

I look up from my oaken desk to see Phineas Lambert walk into the office. There's an impish grin on his face as he comes up to me. "I'm sorry that I'm late, sir."

"Sorry you're late?" I say while raising an eyebrow. "Should I terminate your employment here?"

"Oh, I don't know," Phineas replies with a smirk. "Let's ask your partner." He turns around once and then says, "Dear sir, shall we let go this man who cannot seem to arrive before ten in the morn'?" He then turns back around. "Nay. He's a goodly fellow with plenty of charm. Keep him around."

I laugh. "You're a damned fool, Phin. Or perhaps I'm the fool for making you partner."

"You knew to what you were subscribing, kind sir." We both laugh as my soliciting partner has a seat across from me. "I've just come from the jail. The shoppe owner is not altogether certain he can appear before the court."

"What do you mean?"

"Honestly, he's not up to dick," Phineas replies. "The man is near looned, James. His mind is foggy and quite confused."

"Bloody hell," I grunt as I shake my head. "The judge won't care. He'll throw him in the hole for the next ten years, Phin. Something has to give with that man."

"The judge or the prisoner?" he asks wryly. I can't help but smile a little as I look at the jovial man sitting across from me.

"The shoppe owner," I reply. "He's put himself into quite a position. How is the breadmaker?"

Phineas shakes his head. "Not well, I'm afraid. It appears that he's lost his sight in one eye and might have lost the use of one hand. He can walk, though. That's some consolation." There was a terrible ruckus between the two men when the breadmaker went over to the shoppe beside his bakery and complained about a line of customers that had formed along the walkway in front of his door. He didn't think his own customers could access his business very well. They argued and traded insults as there had already been old wounds between the two of them when the incident occurred. Soon, both men were trading blows, the shoppe owner getting the best of his opponent as he brought a crashing blow against the left side of the other man's head. It caused what appears to be a stroke that has robbed some of the breadmaker's physical faculties from him.

"Ten years at the least. It could be life, though. The breadmaker will likely not be able to return to his vocation." I shake my head. "You need to convince the shoppe owner to stand and defend himself. He needs to make known that the other man came to him to start the fight. It's his only chance." Unlike the poor man that I defended yesterday before the judge, the shoppe owner has money. We are being paid very well to give him our best legal advice and he should take it as gospel. If he does not, his life beyond the grey walls of a prison could be forfeit.

"You should speak with him," Phineas replies. "He refuses to listen to me. I'm growing tired of battling his tongue." My soliciting partner shakes his head. "We can't force him to speak on his own behalf, my friend. No, methinks he'll simply allow himself to be forever condemned as the sole aggressor."

"Damned fool," I growl as I strike my fist upon my desk lightly.

"I have other news, however," Phineas tells me. "I've a new lover."

I roll my eyes. "You shouldn't Phin. You know that if your wife catches you it will be an arduous divorce."

"A *divorce?* She would never," he chuckles. "Katherine is far too fond of the finer things to let me go."

"You are taking an extreme risk, sir. You have been married far too long to continue this tomfoolery with other ladies."

"Lorena is simply too much, James. You should meet her." He smiles broadly as he speaks of his new lover. "She's Slovenian, you know."

"Slovenian?" I laugh. "How did you come upon a Slovenian woman?"

"She's a dancer in a show in Portsmouth."

"Very dangerous, Phineas," I tell him. "Katherine is no fool."

"She's what I want her to be," Phineas replies. "Do you think she cares what I do when I take my trips? Of course not. She likely has her own cock to keep warm whilst I'm away."

"Sir." My cheeks blush a little as I shake my head and look around. There are no clients in the office at this time and the other solicitors are appearing in court this morning.

Phineas leans toward my desk and smiles. "Lorena warms my cock nicely, James. Does Emma do as much for you?"

"Please, Phin," I say while shaking my head. "We shouldn't be speaking of such things in this place."

"Why not?" he questions. "It is our cocks that need the most attention, aye? My cock has become thirsty with Katherine and so I have been forced to find other fine quim. Lorena provides such comfort, my fellow." Phineas smiles wickedly as he leans back in his seat. "Some might even refer to the sweet woman as a blowsy."

My face turns color again. "Is she?"

My partner grins and wags his head from one side to the other. "Some might think so, certainly. Lorena's skills are multifaceted, James. You should see her at work." He laughs as he watches me shake my head and turn even redder by the moment. Phineas knows that I'm not much for the sort of conversation he enjoys. No, my preference is to speak of things that either concern the law or polite society.

"Katherine..."

"Katherine be damned," he snorts. "She's brought this upon herself, James. Do you take her as someone who pleases her husband? No. She does not. It's natural that a man like me would seek out such comforts if his own wife cannot provide them."

I swallow hard. "Emma can be cold to the touch sometimes as well," I tell him. I've not spoken to Phineas about such things before, but I'm beginning to think that I should. Especially in light of his interests.

"They all can," he admits. "However, have things gotten so that you wish for a lover as well?"

"Outside of wedlock?" I shake my head. "I love her deeply, Phin. She's my Irish princess."

"Ah, the Irish *princess,*" he chuckles. "You fell in love with her pearly voice, didn't you?"

"She is more than her accent, sir," I reply brusquely. "Please keep that in mind."

My partner raises his hands to his chest and nods his head. "I understand. Please know that I mean nothing untowards to your lovely wife, James."

My heart beats hard for a moment as I consider the life that Phineas is living with his wife and separate Slovenian lover. Though he shouldn't be so quick to admit to anyone that he has taken a lover outside his home, he knows that I am completely trustworthy. Speaking of such things to others isn't likely on my part, which means that I'm a safe sounding board for my soliciting partner. Even so, he knows that these conversations bother me more than just a little. Phineas seems to enjoy putting me back on my foot with surprising revelations regarding his private life.

"Katherine will not put her mouth on it, James," he tells me as he motions to his trousers front. "I have pleaded with her to do as much over the years, but she has often told me that to do so is a mortal sin." Phineas frowns. "Would it honestly be so terrible for her to lick my maypole and ballocks?"

"Phin," I say while shaking my head. "It's a wonder that a lady of Katherine's station hasn't pushed you for a divorce simply because of your vulgar language."

"The money," he replies. "She knows more than she would reckon to any one soul. I told you before that Katherine keeps her own company."

"And you're agreeable to such an arrangement?"

"Wholly and absolutely, my friend," he laughs. "Why wouldn't I be so inclined? I have Lorena and her predilection to ballocks." Phineas laughs and I find myself doing the same as I look away for a moment. It's hard to believe that such a man practices the art of law in front of judges. If he were found out, it would certainly mean the end of his bar membership. The court is not forgiving when it comes to how solicitors and barristers present themselves before judges. We have a reputation to uphold and that reputation is often more valuable than the men who carry it forward.

"Is she lovely? Lorena?"

"Very," he replies. "Would you like to see her? I could bring her to our office for a visit soon."

"No," I answer quickly. "That's not necessary and very probably not advisable."

"But, she's very enamoured with the wares of men, James. I'd wager that she would like to see yours as well."

"She's *your* lover," I reply. "Not mine."

"Ah, but I don't mind allowing her a bit of fun with you, dear fellow. It's all in fun, right?" My face turns red again as I look away from Phineas. Is he actually offering his lover to me for my own bedding? My cock hardens as I give thought to such an idea.

"Do not bring the Slovenian quim here," I tell him. "She's not to step foot inside lest someone sees her and knows the score, Phin. Swear this to me." I look hard at my soliciting partner and await his response.

"Alright," he answers while nodding his head. "Lorena shall not come to the office. Still, you should meet her soon."

"No, I think that would not be very wise," I tell him. "My troubles with Emma would multiply if she caught me doing as much." If I were honest with my partner, I would say to Phineas that I would very much like to meet his lover. However, that would not be in line with my social obligations. Though Emma gives less and less in our private times together, I am nonetheless bonded to her by holy matrimony. This means that I will always be faithful to her, regardless of my partner's own private life of adultery.

"You are an honourable man, sir. Very honourable." Phineas smiles as he stands to his feet. "If you will excuse me, I have work to do. The shoppe owner will need me to be quick witted if he's to be saved from the hole. James, if you happen to think of something, please let me know. His life hangs in the balance." My soliciting partner nods his head to me and smiles before turning and walking away from my desk. He makes his way to the other side of the office and has a seat at his own desk.

My mind wanders again as I consider how cold the intimacy in my marriage to Emma has recently become. There is a great deal of love between us, but unfortunately that love is less than I need many days. The physical component of our life together has been lacking for some time, and soon I fear that it will cause a great strain upon our nuptials. I love Emma Hutchins much more than life itself, but my loins ache for the gentle touch of her soft fingers. There was a time when she would grip my pipe in a way that would cause me to erupt in showers over and over again. That time has come and gone, replaced by a coupling between us that is more traditional and very straightforward. She lies back and I penetrate her. I stream my seed into her wet cavern and then we roll away from each other and go to sleep. We both need and deserve so much more in our bed chamber.

"James, I would hope that your mind is not on my Lorena," I hear Phineas joke from the other side of the office. He circles the fingers on his hand with his thumb and lifts them to his mouth, his lips open in a strained circle. I get the meaning as I watch him move his hands to and from his lips. Yes, I would love to have his secret Slovenian lover drink my nectar. However, this is not to be. I'm a faithful and honourable husband to Emma. I shall always be as much.

Chapter Four: Lest Someone Should See

I'm quiet this evening as Emma and I enjoy dinner together. The footman, Rodney, as well as the housemaid, Claira, are both in the dining room and standing to either side of the dining table. I look at them and nod my head. "Please leave us and retire to your rooms," I tell the two of them. They each bow and move toward the door of the dining room.

Emma looks at me with surprise. "Why have you dismissed the help, James? Is something the matter?"

I take a deep breath and smile softly at her. "I wish to have this time with you alone, my dear," I answer my wife. "We rarely have the opportunity to share our thoughts freely in here."

My Irish wife scoffs. "We have nothing to fear with the likes of Claira or Rodney. They could certainly stay and hear whatever it is that you want to say to me." She smiles at me and I feel the hairs on my neck stand up. Those green eyes. They have cast a spell upon me from the moment I first saw them. Unfortunately, we have forgotten what it is like to truly enjoy each other's company in a strictly carnal vein.

"Perhaps your cloven inlet needs attention, Emma?"

Her eyes grow large. "You would not speak to me in such a way, would you?" she asks in her thick Irish tone.

"My love," I reply. "It's been ages since I last ran my fingers through your downy spring moss." I chuckle as I raise a glass of wine to my lips and take a sip.

My wife's face turns bright red as she looks around the room. "Your tongue has become foul, kind sir. Perhaps it should be cleansed with a proper soap and some water." She suddenly understands why I have dismissed the help from our midst.

"The golden water of your sweet lotus?" I ask with a wicked grin. "Emma, you and I are as one in the eyes of all. We are married. Surely we may speak freely to one another?"

"In our bedchambers," she retorts. "Only there and nary another spot in this house." Emma glares at me. "Did you speak to that cousin of yours? Is he the one from whom you've gained this vulgar speech?"

I chuckle. "Phineas is a good man," I reply. "He did not put me up to this, my love. I can assure you of as much." I stand to my feet and walk toward my beautiful wife. My cock becomes hard as I make my way to her and she notices the bulging trousers.

"The bedchambers," she repeats. "Only there and only when the sun has fallen from the sky. James, don't do this here."

"Do what?" I reply as I come close to her. I press my hardness against her arm as she sits still in her chair. Emma doesn't know what to do as I press into her. "This is yours, my love. Would you like to enjoy a taste of it?"

Her face turns up as she looks back at me. *"Vulgar,"* Emma replies in her Irish accent. "It's no way to treat a fine lady," she tells me. "Go find a whore if that is your desire."

"Oh, I have already found my whore." I reach down and take hold of my wife's hand and help her to her feet. Her eyes grow wide as I push her over the table. "What are you doing, James? This isn't proper or respectable."

"It's both and yet even more," I say as I pull at her bloomers. They fall to her feet and her sweet backside is now easy to see. I look at her long, musky crack and think about how she must taste. It's the sort of thing that I have longed for over the years; to taste her bushy folds. Emma allowed this on our wedding night, as she believed it to be customary for the man to have his way in all respects concerning his wife. Since then, however, she has sat and gossiped with her highbred friends and they've instilled in her the notion that only plain, penetrative copulation should be performed between a man and his wife. Other things belong in a brothel in the company of whores and lesser men. Not among those of privileged upbringing.

"James, this is not proper," she tells me as I open my trousers and pull out my hard pole. It's already wet on the tip as I push it toward her tight cavern. As I enter her, Emma shakes and continues to protest. "Not right, James. Not right at all." Her accent is much thicker now and I wonder if she's about to speak in Irish Gaelic to me. Emma has done so before when she's gotten a bit frustrated with me.

"You're like a clenched fist," I moan as I move back and forth inside her soft, wet notch. It has been at least two weeks since we last enjoyed each other's company in this way, and it was in very much the same form and fashion as it always seems to be; with her on her back and her legs open in the dark of night. I look down and smile as I see my hard pole sliding easily in and out of her bushy muff.

"James, pull out and at least allow me the dignity of the bed," Emma growls. "Don't do this. It's so uncouth."

"It's not uncouth," I reply as I enjoy the feeling of her hole surrounding my shagging pole. "Woman, you're going to cause me to spill my seed into your furrow." My ballocks ache for the release of my white sauce into Emma as I move faster. My hands take hold of her soft, round buttocks and I pull my wife to me hard. We collide in a loud clapping sound that probably reaches as far as the private quarters of the hired help. I do not care, though. Right now all I want is to enjoy the soft nape of Emma's fertile fruit.

"Oh, James. No. *Stop.*" Her body rocks a little back and forth as she begins to grind into me. I've seen this before with my wife. There are times when she also experiences a climax of passion. Phineas tells me that this is normal in women, though I often wonder. Emma often eschews such feelings as sinful and beneath her station. Worthy of lowly whores, she has told me on more than one occasion.

"I won't stop," I tell her as I feel my ballocks pushing my seed toward my erect pole. "I will empty myself into you, my love. All of me." My breathing becomes faster as I clench my teeth tightly together.

"James...*ahhhhh...*" Emma buries her face into her hands as she begins to enjoy the presence of my cock so deeply buried inside her. *"Mmmmm...MMMMMM..."* My wife keeps her face covered as her sweet flower becomes wet with her passion.

"Emma, it's alright. It's...*ohhhh...OHHHH!!!*" My seed is pushed hard into her deep hole as I shove my pole deep into her. *"Emma. OHHHHH, Emma. FUCK...FUCK!!!"* I can't believe that I would say such a word in polite company, but I don't care. Emma is my wife and if I want to say *fuck* while we *fuck,* I certainly will. *"Uhhhh..."* I ache with passion for my beautiful wife as I drain myself into her tight cunt. *"Emma...ohhhh..."*

After I finish with her, I pull out of my wife and then look down at my dripping cock. The deed is done and now I will likely pay for my terrible manners with her. After stepping back, I pull up my trousers and button them before straightening my shirt.

Emma pulls up her bloomers and then drops her dress back down over her shame. She allows a quick look at me as she stands beside the table. "You said a terrible word in my presence, James," she begins quietly. "It's the sort of word that is never used in polite company. It doesn't matter whose company you keep."

Looking nervously into her green eyes, I reply, "It's a *word,* Emma. Nothing but a word and I'm not sorry for saying it between us in private. No one heard us."

She shakes her head. "You have treated me like a common whore, James. It's not a small thing. There are things that are allowed, and then there are things that are not. How could you dare to do such a thing to me on our dining table? To say such a foul thing too?"

Shaking my head, I can't help but to laugh a little. "You're far too concerned about a little word like that? *Fuck?*"

Emma shrinks back as she grits her teeth. "Say it again and you will find yourself not in my bed," she threatens. "Is it your intention to put a hedge between us, James?" Her eyes waver as they look from me to the dining room table. "You've soiled our home and our table. We shall never enjoy a dinner party here again."

"Why not?" I ask as I begin to wonder whether Phineas has the right idea with his secret lover.

Emma shakes her head and waves her hands over the top of the wooden table. "You've had your way with me upon it! Why would I serve anyone on this very table now that it's been a part of such a thing, James? It's so vulgar! So...*scannalach!*"

I nod my head. "I thought you might decide to find your Irish tongue for this. You know I don't understand it, my love."

"You understand enough," she retorts. Emma's green eyes focus on me as she shakes her head. "I thought you a much greater gentleman than this, James Hutchins. I can see I was blindly misled." My wife turns and walks toward the dining room doorway. Though I open my mouth to say something in hopes of stopping her, I find my tongue to be somewhat paralyzed.

After a moment of quiet inside the dining room, I sit down in my chair and look around the room. It does seem quite empty and too quiet without Emma and the servants in here with me. What I've done this evening could be my last time with my love for some time.

"Sir?" Rodney pokes his head in through the doorway. "Would you like for me to clean up?" I nod my head and wave the young man in. He is followed by Claira. "We noticed the lady making her way to her room, so we decided we should come out and see what we should do."

"Thank you, Rodney," I say as I nod my head and smile. "It seems that I have offended my wife this evening."

"I'm very sorry, sir." He picks up my plate and wine glass as Claira does the same at Emma's end of the dinner table. "Hopefully all will be better by sunrise."

"Hopefully so," I agree. I wait for Claira to take her handful of dishes from the room before calling out to Rodney. "Just a moment. Please." My heart pounds as he walks back over to where I am sitting.

"I would like to ask you something that must never pass your lips to another, Rodney."

He nods his understanding. "Of course, sir."

I take a breath. "What is your take on the word *fuck?"* I say this quietly so as to avoid offending Claira's young ears. It is, after all, a vulgar word.

The footman's eyes grow wide as he looks from me to the door that leads to the kitchen. Turning back to me, he replies, "I've heard it before, sir, but not more than thrice."

"Ah." I nod my head. "Is it really that terrible? Would it offend most men of your station?"

Rodney presses his lips together tightly before answering. "It would be offensive in most situations, Mr. Hutchins. The word means something rather...intimate."

"Of course," I say quickly. "I'm aware of the meaning." I can see that I need to be more specific. "I spoke it in error to Mrs. Hutchins and I'm afraid that I might have offended her greatly." There was quite a lot more that happened between us, but that's not something I wish to share with the help at this moment.

"I see." He nods his head. "Many ladies would not know it's meaning to begin with, but if she does then it means that she's already heard it once or more. Mr. Hutchins, there are laws against such vocabulary."

"I'm very aware," I answer. There are at least three laws in Southampton that I could quote in general concerning the usage of such volatile language. To simply say *fuck* to one's wife in private would likely not trigger any of them. However, to allow it to slide from one's own tongue in public would likely lead to the lash. It would be a fate similar to or even far worse than that assigned to Mr. Crowley just the other day.

"It would be better that you not use it so freely," Rodney advises me as he nods his head and turns to walk toward the door of the kitchen.

As he leaves, I think about what I've said and done in Emma's presence. If her father knew the cad I had become, he might be tempted to wrest her from my home and take her back to Dublin with him. It's not the sort of thing that I would want to happen. Not for a four letter word of ill repute.

I turn and walk toward the doorway that leads to the parlor. I need a smoke from my pipe and a glass of sherry to wash down the letters that still flutter around inside my mouth. Perhaps it will help to keep me from uttering such terrible things again. I can only hope that Emma will find it in her heart to forgive me for being so incredibly thick-headed with her. It will likely mean that I will have to swear to keep my cock inside my pants while in the dining room from this time hence. Hopefully I can make and keep such a vow to her.

Chapter Five: An Old Acquaintance

My wife has spoken little to me in the last three days since I put myself upon her in the dining room of our home. I thought it would awaken something within my lovely Emma, but alas, there has been nary a glance in my direction from her since that time. I ache for her attention and affection, but I'm afraid that I have pushed her too far away by having my way with her. I have begun to doubt her commitment to me in this marriage.

"Greetings, friends!" The middle-aged man at the door smiles as he steps past his butler and outstretches his hands. I take hold of his hand and shake it before he turns his attention to Emma and smiles. He brings her hand to his mouth and kisses it gently before saying, "I grew concerned when I did not receive a formal reply to my invitation. I was equally thankful when the errand boy brought a note in the affirmative this morning, though." Gray Stokes is a man in his fifties who has never married. A consummate bachelor, he enjoys his solitude at times, but then again looks forward to such soirees as the one he has put together for this evening.

"We apologize for the oversight," Emma says as she smiles kindly at him. "We have been very busy recently and should have answered you sooner. I do hope that you forgive us."

Gray smiles widely. "1873 has been an odd year, in more respects than one." The older gentleman has a great wit when it comes to conversation, which is one reason why I enjoy so much coming to his home. "All is forgiven, forgotten, and, well...you know the rest." He moves to the side to allow us into his home. "Please walk the room and visit with others as you will. A light meal will be served as we enjoy the company of all." Gray bows his head slightly before turning and walking toward the kitchen.

"It's nice to be here," I say to my wife as we walk into the large room full of people. All are social animals, yapping away as if they are puppies who have been gathered into the same cage. I smile as I see several of our acquaintances nearby.

"Nice. Yes." Emma's cold reply is a testament to her resiliency when it comes to verbally whipping at me. Perhaps I'm a cad for what I did and said in our dining room, but she comes across as a cold bitch when she treats me thusly.

We approach a small group of young men and women who are in conversation. They stop and greet us. "Good evening, James. Good evening, Emma," Mrs. Louisa Wellings says to us. "It's wonderful to see the both of you." She offers her hand and I reach out to take hold of it before kissing it. Emma smiles and gently shakes her hand. "I believe you know Mr. Kerry Thornton, III and Ms. Abigail Lane?"

"We know them, yes." I shake Kerry's hand and then kiss the young Ms. Lane's hand. Emma trades pleasantries with them as well as I look on. Kerry's blue eyes focus on my wife for a moment before he turns them toward me. He quickly looks away, seemingly knowing that I've noticed his gawking.

"And, are the two of you currently..." Emma points to Kerry and Abigail."

"Oh, heavens, no," Abigail says while turning bright pink. "We are close cousins, you see. We grew up together in Lancashire."

"Really? We've known you both for some time and have never been told as much," I say with a chuckle.

"I am deeply sorry for the confusion," Emma tells them. "Honestly, deeply sorry."

"'Tis no harm," Kerry replies cheerfully. "We have been mistaken as such before now, and we will likely be so again." He laughs with us as my wife's face turns deep red. I watch as her green eyes look at the young man. There is almost something between them. I can feel it as I study their faces. Emma would think me vulgar if I were to look at another woman in this same way.

"So, have you seen any of your old school chums around here?" Mrs. Wellings asks as she smiles at me. She, too, appears to have noticed Emma's flagrant eye contact with the young man.

"Not as of yet," I reply as I look over at her. "We have just arrived."

"I see." She nods her head. "Emma, I would guess that the soup kitchen is doing well?" The older woman is aware of my wife's charity work in a soup kitchen that is funded by the higher born in society.

Emma turns to look at her. "All is well there," she tells her. "The donations have been generous this year and I feel that we are going to have a wonderful Christmas celebration for those in need."

"It's still three months away," I say to her. "And yet, you're already planning?"

A sort of retributory raise of her eyebrow tells me that my wife isn't happy with my interjection into the conversation. "We plan ahead, sir." The answer to my query is as cold as her attitude toward me has been these last three days.

"And I'm sure it will be a grand event." Kerry smiles at us both. "I would love the opportunity to help with any arrangements that are yet to be made. There are plenty of servants in my house who could come and help as well." Again, his blue eyes seem to dance in his head as he looks at my wife. There is definitely something between them. I can see it. What is it that they see in each other?

"We are well appropriated and maintained," Emma replies. "However, I would be most grateful for any help that is given, sir. I will send word when we begin the major tasks for the Christmas dinner and celebration."

"Those less fortunate will become most fortunate that day, I am certain." Kerry nods his head a little as he smiles.

"Well. I think I shall retreat to the wine table, my friends. Abigail, would you like to join me?" I can see that Mrs. Wellings has decided to withdraw herself from whatever is happening here. I can't blame her, and I wish I could vanish as well. However, I have a duty to stay with my wife, no matter the thoughts that must be bouncing around inside her beautiful head.

I watch as the two women leave our little group. Then, I say to my wife and Kerry, "They say that there will be a lively group of men coming through Southampton in the spring."

"Oh?" Kerry turns to look at me.

"Certainly. There are repairs to be made to the old courthouse and they have hired a London outfit to do the work. At least a hundred men will advance on the location and begin repairs and renovation work."

"A hundred men?" Emma shakes her head. This is the first time she has heard of this from me. Honestly, I consider the information a bit mundane for her tastes in general.

"The project is to be completed in two weeks. The judges want as little upset to the court schedule as possible." Looking over at Kerry, I ask, "Isn't this an area of expertise for your own family, sir?"

He smiles and nods his head. "It 'tis, James. However, we rarely bid for work that is of the public nature. Most of my family's involvement is in the restoration of private estates." The Thornton family has a long reputation as consummate builders, going back at least three centuries in England. Their wealth is built upon the fact that they have had a storied and long connection to the higher born families, especially around London. They are respected as much as any other builder.

"We should consider renovating our home," Emma says with a smile as she looks at me. Her eyes cast upon me for a moment before she turns them to gaze once again at the young man in our trio. "Would you do work in Southampton, sir?"

"Aye, I would be grateful for the opportunity, madam." He nods his head and grins, a dimple appearing on his cheek. Though at first I consider trying to wipe said dimple from his face, I begin to enjoy the stares they exchange. Is it lust that they feel? A human desire to copulate...adulterate...behind my back? My mind imagines what it would be like to catch the two of them in mid-coitus, my wife's back arched along the bed as young, virile Kerry thrusts his shaft deep into her waiting well of sweetness. My cock stiffens slightly at the thought and I quickly shake myself from it. To have such a mind is undoubtedly less than gentlemanly on my part.

"Thankfully, we do not have need of any work at this time," I offer as I look at the two of them. "Emma simply enjoys the thought of things being different from time to time. I know I do." My wife quickly gets the reference and blushes as she considers the time in the dining room three evenings prior. I have begged her for different things in our time in the bed chamber, only for Emma to refuse. Is it really so terrible that a man would like to enjoy every part of his beautiful wife? Can I not bed her in the manner that so many men are bedding their women daily?

"I see," Kerry replies as he looks nervously at us. "I think I should retire to the wine table myself. Please excuse me." He bows slightly toward Emma and takes her hand, kissing it lightly, before nodding to me and turning to leave us.

My wife seethes. "Do you intend to embarrass me this evening?" Emma asks as she looks around the room, feigning gladness to be in my presence.

"Of course you are angry," I chuckle. "I've interrupted his preening."

"His *preening?"* Emma looks hard at me. "What do you mean by that, James?"

I shrug my shoulders. "His eyes could not keep from you, my dear. It is obvious that he has some affection for you. Where do you suppose he has found such affection?"

"Affection?" Emma frowns. "Are you accusing me of infidelity, husband?"

"No, of course not," I answer. "Never would I do anything of the sort." I am certain that there has been no physical contact between her and the young Kerry Thornton, III. However, there was definitely a knowing of some sort between the pair. The give and take visually was unmistakable.

"If you are going to accuse me, James..."

"I'm not accusing anyone of anything," I say quietly to her as I look around the room. "On the contrary, my love. I have been imagining him buried up to his ballocks inside your soft wool."

Emma's face turns pale and then bright red. "How could you say such a thing? And here? James, it's a caddish thing that you consider. Pray that it is erased from your thoughts."

"I pray that Kerry feasts upon your sweet tulip, my love. I would pay for any renovation on our home if you would allow him such an honor." I swallow hard as I smile broadly. My cock, hard and leaking, is beginning to show through my trousers and Emma can see the bulge.

"Take it down," she says while looking at my trousers with wide eyes. Emma attempts to stand between me and anyone who might have a look at the monster growing inside. "Take it down this instant, James."

"I can't take it down," I reply with a wicked chuckle. "Perhaps you would like to milk it for me, eh?" Though I've had nothing to drink, I act as if I'm a man drunken with some form of madness. My lust is on full display, and I haven't a care in the world. All I want is to see Kerry bed my wife.

"You're...*vulgar!*" Emma steps back and then turns to walk away. I watch as she goes to the wine table and stops there beside Abigail and the others. Turning, I attempt to keep my swelling cock to myself. Willing it to go down will not be easy this evening. There are too many things on my mind to consider relaxing my masculine constitution. No, this will likely require a visit to the water closet in order to abate my current physical encumbrance.

Chapter Six: A Fine Pub

"A message for you, sir." The boy hands me a note as I stand just inside my office door. I look around at the horses and buggies passing by as I open the folded note. Turning my attention to it, I begin to read the few words on the single page.

"Come to The Red Lion for lunch. Noon."

The note is signed by Kerry Thornton, III. I look up and ask the boy, "From whence did this come?"

He nodded down the street. "A man gave it to me and offered sixpence to deliver it." I can see by his open hand that the messenger would like some more money, so I reach into my pocket and find a few pennies that I drop into his hand. Delighted, he turns and runs off alongside the carriage traffic.

"The Red Lion," I muse to myself as I walk back into my office and sit down. Being that now it is half-past eleven, I will soon have to make the trip to the pub if I'm going to go at all. But then again, why has Kerry asked me to come to him? What has he on his mind? Though I struggle to convince myself otherwise, I know deep inside my soul that this has something to do with Emma. Perhaps he wishes to offer his tradesmanship again, this time man to man? "Perhaps," I say under my breath. I don't believe it, though.

"You appear deep in thought, James," Phineas says as he walks up to my desk. "Care to share your mind?"

I shake my head. "I've a meeting with a gentleman at The Red Lion."

"Oh? Anyone with whom I am acquainted?" My cousin is always hungry for more information than he deserves. I'll allow him a tidbit for now.

"Kerry Thornton," I reply. "Of the Thornton building firm in London."

"London? Why in Heaven's name would he be here in Southampton?"

"Just an old friend wishing to visit," I reply. Getting up from my desk I nod and smile at Phineas. "Can you hold out here without me for a time?"

"Certainly," he replies while raising an eyebrow. "Will this Mr. Thornton be requiring the counsel of our office?"

"No," I say as I shake my head. "He's well managed, I'm certain."

"Ah, good. Still, if you would like to drop my name, I just lost a client myself."

"You *lost* a client? How did you lose a client?" In my mind, Phineas is probably talking about someone who has decided to no longer retain our services. However, this quickly becomes obvious to not be the case.

"The poor bugger hanged himself evening last." I'm shocked at how calmly my soliciting partner delivers this news to me.

"Hanged?"

"With a long rope he purchased from a local smithy. The constabulary surmised he passed quickly, though. Bless his wife and child." Phineas shakes his head as he presses his lips hard together.

"The client who was charged with indecency?" My partner nods his head. "Oh, my. That will likely cause the judge to rule against him."

"His family will suffer for this happenstance. I had cautioned him against any rash actions, but apparently the guilt finally overtook him."

I sigh. "He was truly at fault, then? For the indecency charge?" Doylan Freeman is the client of which we speak. He was a common laborer who moved from job to job as he was needed. Though not a wealthy man, he appeared to have taken admirable care of his wife and children. Someone reported, however, that he liked to pleasure himself in the dark places near where the social elites sometimes come together. He was caught by one young lady while spilling his seed upon the ground.

"The local charities will not take kindly to the woman or her children, I'm afraid. The father's sins and all that." Phineas shakes his head. "Enjoy the pub. I hear they serve a wonderful meal of fish at midday." He smiles and nods his head before going back to his desk. I leave the office and begin my walk to where I will meet with Kerry Thornton.

I walk in just before noon to find only a half-dozen people in the old pub. As I look around the room, I don't recognize anyone at first. However, Kerry's hand goes up and I see where he's sitting. I move to join him at his table.

"Hello, friend," he says to me as he stands to his feet and offers his hand. We shake. "Please have a seat." We both sit down and I look over at him as I wonder what this is all about.

"I suppose you've decided to stay in Southampton for a time?" I ask as I sit back in my chair.

Kerry nods his head. "For a short time, aye. 'Tis a nice place to visit."

"It is," I reply. The silence that quickly develops between us is nearly unbearable.

"Well, I think I should get to it then, eh?" He smiles at me as his face turns bright pink. "About the evening we last spoke," Kerry begins. "I hope you feel no offense was intended on my part concerning your lovely wife, Emma."

My heart beats hard as I think about the way I spoke to my marital partner at the dinner party. "No offense on my part, no," I say as a woman approaches our table with two pints of dark stout.

"I hope this meets to your satisfaction," Kerry says before handing the woman a coin. She nods and walks away.

"Drink is always acceptable," I reply as I pick up the glass and hold it toward him. "No offense."

"No offense." Our glasses lightly clack together before we each take a drink. As we put the glasses down on the scarred table, Kerry tells me, "I find Emma to be a very handsome woman, sir. Although I understand that this statement might find disfavor in her husband, I want to make that point clear."

My cock hardens a little. "A *handsome* woman?"

"Very," he replies. "In as much as I would like to make an offer that I hope you might find equally attractive." The man's blue eyes feel as if they are burrowing into me as he speaks.

"Go on." Though a part of me would enjoy striking the other man for what I know is going through his thoughts, I decide to wait to hear his offer.

Kerry leans toward the table and says in hushed tone, "I would like very much to bed your wife while you watch." His blue eyes continue to look into mine as he sits back again. There is no doubt in his expression as to the veracity of his desire to know Emma carnally.

"You can't be serious."

"Oh, but I am," he replies with a devilish smirk. "James, I could see it in you that evening as plain as we are sitting here; you wish the same. You want your sweet Emma to be soiled by another." His words are thorny as he addresses me concerning my wife. Why would another man make such evil intentions known? Kerry does not know me well enough to know that I would not strike him for less than what he suggests to me now.

I take a quick breath. "Emma would never consider such a thing. She's a proper lady and she would never let another man cow her into going to her back for him."

"Her back. Her knees. Does she like to nibble on a gentleman's swollen nob occasionally?"

"Great heavens, Kerry. Your tongue is filthy." My face continues to burn red as I try to determine what I shall do with the man across the table from me.

"I'm aware of as much," he chuckles. His smile disappears for a moment. "I was married, James. You met her once. Glenda was her name."

"A lovely woman," I say as I slowly turn the glass of stout on the table with my fingers.

"Taken too soon," he replies. "Yet, even while in marital bliss, she understood my needs. My desires."

My face becomes hot. "She *knew?*"

"She did," Kerry admits. "And she approved. James, even a woman needs to know other lovers on the occasion. I am that other lover that your Emma needs and desires. Allow this and I can guarantee that she will want you even more."

"She's a prudish hen," I quickly retort. I'm shocked by the speed with which I have offered such criticism of Emma to another man. "She would never allow you to have your way with her."

"And yet, you have offered such to her?" he asks. I nod my head. "She is the type of woman who is only comfortable when the man is in control and on top. Is that a fair assessment, James?" Again, I nod my head. I do not understand how I continue to entertain this conversation, but I do. All while my manly meat grows and moves inside my trousers.

"Emma is a proper wife," I tell him. "One who is modest, yet loving. She gives as she needs to give and expects the same in return. I cannot find fault in her for as much."

"Yet, you want much more." Kerry smiles. "I know you, sir. I've seen your kind over and over again. Your wife is dutiful and will submit to you, but only while abiding with her notions of what is proper and ladylike. Fucking like dogs is never allowed." There is that word. The one that I used copiously during intercourse with my fair maiden in our dining room. Emma despises that word and would quickly remove herself from the presence of any man who employs such linguistic perversion.

"Perhaps I do want more from my wife," I answer carefully. "There are many men in the same predicament, I would wager. Good men. Men of character. It is our lot in life to be better than the common street urchin, Mr. Thornton. If we do not, we become as mere animals."

"We *are* animals," he answers with a brief laugh. "Surely you've read the latest science. Everything about our kind screams out *animal.* We should then fuck like them, too." Kerry smiles widely as he looks around the pub. I do the same, concerned that his vulgar tongue could endanger us in such a public environment. The local police will not understand our use of the word in polite company. Though, the only others in the pub at this moment are likely not the most polite sort and have heard it all before.

"I don't know..."

"All I request is that you give consideration to my proposition," he tells me before drinking down his stout in one long gulp. After putting the empty glass down, he adds, "You may watch, James. I have offered as much to other men when I have helped their wives to become more...open."

"More open?"

"More open to your desires, James. You see, I am very adept at helping women become willing to do whatever their men want whenever they want. I offer this to you, free of monetary recompense, of course."

"Of course," I reply sarcastically.

"All you have to do is let me know your decision." Kerry reaches into his coat pocket and pulls out a small slip of paper. "This is where I will be staying for the rest of the week. On Saturday evening, I will return to London and to the grind of managing my building firm. I would very much appreciate some time with Emma before I depart. That is, if you are of a mind to watch and enjoy." The young man winks at me before getting up from the table. He then lays money onto the table and leaves me to my thoughts.

"Another man with Emma," I remark quietly as I allow the thought to fill my head. I'm hard as I think this through. "Yes, I could see that." I smile to myself as I pick up my glass of stout and begin to drink again. Seeing Emma with another man would be something very exciting for me. Though, I'm not sure it will be so for her. It will take some shrewd manipulation to get my wife to approve.

Chapter Seven: Prudish Wife

"James." I look up as my soliciting partner calls out to me from the office door. Next to him stands my wife, Emma.

"We need to speak, James," she tells me as she walks toward my desk.

Phineas nods his head. "I'll go to the pub a bit early today, James. See you in the morning." I quickly acknowledge my cousin with a smile before turning my attention back to my wife.

"Emma."

"This," she says to me without explaining beforehand. "Read it."

"Yes, my love." I take the note from her and unfold it before reading the words upon its page.

"Emma, please forgive my forwardness, but I find you to be incredibly sensual. Would you honor me by spending an evening with me at my home? I realize this is most unseemly, but my loins burn for you. I assure you, the woolen lips 'neath your navel will purr with each stroke of my fleshy rod." The note is signed by Kerry Thornton.

"Um..." I look up at Emma, her green eyes sharp as she glares at me.

"He's a terrible cad, James. There are penalties for the likes of him, are there not?" I can see that my wife is meaning that she would like to seek legal recourse against the other man.

"My dear, how did you receive this note?"

She presses her lips hard together before answering, "A young lad of about twelve delivered it to our door not an hour ago. I came straight here to see you about this cruel injustice."

"Cruel?" I shake my head. "How can you be certain that it's from Mr. Thornton, Emma? He's a man of character and standing in his community." I know better. Kerry spoke to me of such things just a day ago. I've tried to put the things he has said out of my mind, but I have given some thought to him lying in bed with Emma. A man of my social standing should be ashamed of his own thoughts, but strangely, I am not.

"His name, plain as day, is on that note, sir," she replies flatly. Her Irish accent has begun to make its appearance as my wife becomes stirred up. "He can't speak to me this way," she argues.

I sigh as I put the note down on my desk. "Emma, I'm not certain I could bring this to the court. The judges are not very receptive to the accusations of ladies toward those of the other sex. Though I understand your anger, I don't know that you..."

"There are *laws* concerning a lady's honour, are there not?" Emma interrupts.

"Well, yes, but normally..."

"Then I want to see him caged as the animal he is," she continues. I should not have to urge you so stoutly, either. You are my husband, James, and I expect you to defend me. Defend my honor." Her eyes continue to stare hard at me as I sigh.

"Would you have me challenge Mr. Thornton to a duel? Perhaps pistols at six in the evening?"

"Is this amusing to you?" Emma growls as she crosses her arms. "You are my husband, are you not? You are a solicitor with clout in the courtroom as well. Bring a case against this animal and see that he pays for his offenses."

"His offenses? Do you mean the offense of being crude in his letter to you? Or that he sent you a letter at all?" I retort. "The court will not be amused, as you say. The judge will laugh at this and then toss the case before scolding me for letting my dear wife press the matter. Furthermore, he will likely charge you the fees for Mr. Thornton's solicitor and court costs. We cannot win this, my love." It has been some time since an English court has used such laws to successfully prosecute a man who has decided to write a salacious note to a married woman. Carelessly send your spittle to the ground before a woman of polite society and be judged. However, these charges would have practically no chance of success if brought before the court.

Emma drops down into a chair on the other side of my desk, her face red. "Why can he not be punished? What he says in that note is not at all seemly."

"As he freely admits in the note," I tell her. "Emma, the problem is that he can always claim to have no knowledge of the note and that you are attempting to blemish his reputation. The court will side with him quickly."

"Because I'm a *woman?"* I nod my head. My wife isn't happy with my response, but I have never been one to lie to her or anyone else when it comes to the complications of our justice system. I am always an open book.

"It was just some playful banter."

"Playful banter?" Emma shakes her head. "You're disgusting for thinking as much, James."

I chuckle. "You're a prude," I reply. "I would wager that Kerry has noticed this and has decided to have a little fun with you by sending the note. It surely means nothing."

Emma narrows her eyes at me. "This is about what I won't do for you, aye?" Her Irish accent is now thick. "You want me to put my mouth on that thing, do you not?"

"That thing?" I smile. "Do you refer to my pole, woman?"

"Your *pole,"* Emma confirms, causing my cock to become long and hard. "Did you send the note to me? Is this a game, James Hutchins?"

"No game," I reply. "However, Kerry is apparently taken by you. He would like to enjoy you in every way that he can carnally." My ballocks ache as I watch the change of expression on my wife's face. Emma has refused practically everything I have asked for while in the bed chamber. She went as far as to kiss my unmentionable on our wedding night, but since then the idea of putting her mouth on it has been considered vile and sinful.

"Did you speak with him?" she asks.

"We spoke," I admit. "Kerry is sincere in wanting to have his way with you. To be very honest, I would not hold him responsible for any fornicatory actions if the both of you fell into each other's arms as I watch." I feel my cock dribble some as I look at my wife across the desk from me. Emma is shocked, as she should be. Her own husband is apparently fine with the thought of his wife allowing another man to plant his seed inside her womb.

After some silence, Emma replies, "You are a vulgar man, James Hutchins. A vulgar, hideous man."

"And you are a prudish hen, strutting yourself before the cockerels from the other side of the fence." The remark sits hard with my beautiful young wife. Though her eyes seem to begin to fill with tears, the tears are soon replaced with rage.

"How dare you? I am your *wife,* and you have vowed to protect me, James. You, above all men on this green earth, have sworn before a priest to hold me in highest regard."

"And you have promised to keep me happy," I flatly announce as I shake my head.

"By allowing you to fill my mouth with your seed?" Emma's face strains into a tight grimace as she shudders. "It's not proper, James. None of what you ask of me in order to make you happy is allowed. The church would certainly find your ideas of happiness less than genteel."

"Aye, perhaps," I say with a chuckle. "But then again, I don't go and talk to Father McMahon about our doings in our own bed." I stare at her, my heart beating solidly inside my chest. Emma is my wife and she's correct in her assessment concerning our vows. I am to protect her. And I do. However, I find my senses filled with the possibilities of my young wife having relations with Mr. Thornton.

"You won't prosecute him, then?" she asks.

"I cannot," I reply. "I'm very sorry, my love. Kerry Thornton is an important man in London and we would quickly find ourselves thoroughly embarrassed."

"You mean that *I* would be embarrassed."

"Of course."

"Then I accept that possibility, James."

"I'm afraid that I cannot." My answer is final, and Emma knows as much. Though I am a fine solicitor, there is no option to take Kerry to court over a matter of a filthy note delivered to her. Besides, I would prefer not that the judges in Southampton municipal court know of such a thing regarding my marital relations.

"*Vulgar.* Good day, Mr. Hutchins." My wife turns and walks toward the door of the office. Phineas stands up from his desk and opens the door for her. Emma walks out and my partner quietly closes the door behind her. He makes his way to my desk.

"Emma seems sorely displeased, James," he says while sitting down nearby.

I nod my head. "More so than you know. It seems that a man we both have as an acquaintance sent her a note that was less than gentlemanly." I pass the paper to Phineas and watch his reaction as he reads the words.

"Did he in fact send this?" he asks.

"It wasn't sent by post, but by a messenger boy. So, no, there really isn't a way to prove that he sent the note. However, Emma wishes for me to prosecute him for lewdness or some other offense. I've told her that doing so would be fruitless."

"Probably," my partner replies. "The question, however, is whether you are offended?" He watches me as I chuckle. Phineas and I have had many unsavory conversations concerning other women, so he understands my mind far too well.

"Of course," I lie. "What sort of cad would I be otherwise?"

Phineas grins and then gets up from his seat. "This is between you and Mrs. Hutchins. Good luck, my friend. You'll need it." He walks back to his own desk and has a seat. I turn back to the note on my desk.

"Dammit, Kerry. Why have you attempted to subvert me? We have discussed this already," I say under my breath. What he told me before at the pub intrigued me and I have even given some consideration to his proposal. However, I need time to ply Emma's mind in a way that she might accept such a thing as well. Sending a note to her in this fashion has made things all the more difficult between us. It will be practically impossible now to convince my wife to go along with Mr. Thornton's proposal.

Chapter Eight: Invitation

"You won't believe this," Phineas says later in the afternoon as he hands me a sealed envelope with Kerry Thornton's seal on the back. "A lad just delivered this for you." He steps back and watches as I open it and unfold the note held within. I read it with surprise.

"Mr. Thornton wishes to see me at his Southampton home concerning the note to my wife."

"Really?" I nod my head and my soliciting partner chuckles. "He's got quite the set of ballocks."

"Very much so," I say with a slight smile. "He states that the note was misinterpreted. Apparently Emma sent him a scathing response this morning after visiting with me."

"Ah. Will you be going to see him, then?"

"Of course," I reply. "It would be less than gentlemanly to do anything less."

"Perhaps. Would you like me to attend as well?"

I shake my head. "Stay here and attend to our business instead. Mr. Thornton and I will have a private conversation about my wife's concerns. If this can be put to rest, it would do well for all involved."

Phineas raises an eyebrow. "You do understand that the note he sent to your wife was very salacious, James? There is no clear path to refute as much."

I smile and pat my partner on the shoulder. "I understand that I wish for things to be more cordial between Kerry Thornton and my wife. Whatever must happen to accomplish as much, I will see to it." I reach for my jacket and hat. "After I see to this meeting, I'll likely go home. Good evening, Phineas."

"Good evening, James." He watches as I leave the office and close the door behind me. A buggy and driver happen to always be stationed nearby. This is a very opportune part of the small city for the likes of these horsemen, and I often take advantage of their offer to transport me. As I hand a coin to the driver, I board the buggy and sit back as he snaps the reigns. The horse begins to trot along the stone street toward the part of town where Mr. Thornton currently resides. It's not a great distance to get there, and the buggy is more than comfortable as the sun begins to set. We arrive in under twenty minutes and I hand the driver another coin. He tips his hat.

"If you'll wait for me here, there will be more than that. I shouldn't be more than an hour, I would think."

"As you wish, sir." He nods at me and sits back in his seat.

I approach the door of the small manor house situated just inside the city limits. As I reach for the door, it suddenly opens and an older gentleman nods his head. "Mr. Hutchins?"

"Aye," I reply in the affirmative.

"Mr. Thornton has been expecting you." He stands to the side and allows me to pass. As I enter the home, he closes the door behind me and says, "I will take you to the parlor. He will see you there." I follow the butler to the small parlor and step inside just before the older man closes the double doors behind me. I'm alone for now, a baby grand piano in one corner of the room and lovely fabric-covered chairs in another. There are books in shelves along the walls and I find myself wondering if Kerry actually reads any of them or if he has had them placed here simply to feign a sense of learnedness to his visitors.

"James," I hear him say from behind me. I turn to see Kerry Thornton walking toward me, his hand outstretched toward me. We take each other's hands and shake before he waves a hand toward a couch nearby. I take a seat just as a young woman in a servant's uniform walks into the room.

"You have a very nice home here, sir," I say as I try to make pleasant conversation.

Kerry smiles. "Thank you very much. Would you like anything? Perhaps some tea?"

"Of course," I answer as I nod my head. Though we have some pressing issues ahead to discuss, I am not the sort of gentleman to refuse such a kind offer.

"Tea, if you please, Sarah." Kerry looks over at the young woman servant. She turns and makes her way to the door and leaves. "She will return soon. Sarah makes excellent black leaf tea."

"Very nice," I reply as I watch my host have a seat in a chair nearby. "So, the note," he begins as he shakes his head. "I'm afraid I wrote that while having a terrible time this morning after a long night of imbibement."

"Oh?" In the times I have seen Kerry at parties and other occasions, not once have I known him to take to the strong drink to the point of drunkenness.

"I would like to give my apology directly to Mrs. Hutchins, but I realize that she might not be receptive to such a gesture."

I chuckle. "You and I had an interesting meeting not long ago, sir. I do not recall that you were under any encumberments while we spoke."

Kerry sighs. "I stand beside my insistence that you both need to be more free, James. It's easy to judge a man such as myself if one does not understand his logic."

"Emma is highly offended, Kerry," I reply. "She came to my office and attempted to convince me that I should prosecute you based on that note to her. It is a fairly damning note, to be certain." The young servant woman walks back into the parlor with a silver service tray that holds a pot of tea as well as some sweets. She places the tray on a table nearby and begins to pour us each a cup.

"As I have already indicated, I would apologize to her personally if it would be appropriate. However, it is not appropriate, as I'm certain you would agree." The young woman hands me a cup of tea and then carries one to Kerry.

"Thank you, Sarah."

"Will there be anything else?" she asks.

Kerry looks at me and then at the young woman. "I need additional service, if you don't mind."

"Certainly, Mr. Thornton." The servant goes to her knees on the floor between his legs and begins to undo his trousers.

"What is this?" I ask as I place my cup back onto its saucer.

"Service," Kerry replies simply. The young woman finds his swelling cock and pulls it out. She runs her hands up and down the length of his girthy manhood twice before putting her mouth over it. My host takes a quick breath before putting his cup of tea to the side on a small table. "Sarah gives excellent service, sir. Unlike any that I have employed before." She pushes his lengthy meat all the way to the back of her throat until his ballocks gently tap her chin. Then the young servant woman lifts her head back up, her lips cradling the head of his large pole before moving back down again. There is no doubt that Kerry enjoys her mouth greatly.

My own snake stiffens as I watch her. "This is highly unusual," I tell him as I strain to keep him from seeing my growing bulge.

"Highly unusual? How so?" Kerry chuckles as he puts a hand on the back of Sarah's head. "She is paid well for her services, sir. Even those services that require her special talents." The man moves around in his chair as he enjoys her soft, wet mouth. At this moment, Emma is the furthest person from my mind. Oh, that Sarah would come to me and service me in like manner!

"This is illegal," I tell him. "You are not married to her, are you?"

"No," Kerry replies. "Nor am I married at all at this time. My wife, quite sadly, is no longer of this world, as you well know, James."

"'Tis fornication," I offer.

The young man laughs. "'Tis *head,*" he replies. "And it is as old as time itself. I am in need of satisfaction from time to time, James, and I have those who give that to me. They are compensated very well, I assure you." His body stiffens. "Sarah, it's coming," he warns her. *"Uhhhh..."* His body convulses lightly as the young woman accepts his seed into her mouth. *"Ohhh...swallow...ohhhhh..."* He continues to spurt his thick soup into the servant's mouth until he finishes. She pulls back and swallows what he has given her, a smile forming on her face afterward. "Good girl," he says to her breathlessly as she puts his cock back into his trousers. Sarah then fastens the front of them before standing to her feet and smiling at Kerry.

"Anything I can do for you, sir?" she asks as she turns and looks toward me.

My face becomes hot. "No, madam, there is not." I swallow hard as I consider what it would be like to receive the same service from the young woman. Though tempting, I know such a thing would not be at all proper. Of course, no part of this afternoon's meeting with Mr. Thornton is proper.

"Very well." She smiles and nods before walking toward the door of the parlor. As she leaves, I turn my attention to the man sitting nearby.

"Your reputation appears to be incomplete," I tell him.

Kerry laughs. "There are things in this world that are considered for public consumption, my friend. While others are less amenable to wandering eyes." Taking the cup of tea into his hand, he continues, "Emma is a fine woman. I have no doubt that her breeding is beyond reproach. However, she seems to be a bit less than accommodating for her husband."

"That is not a subject for you..."

"I mean no harm by the observation," he interrupts. "However, a man should have the option of such pleasures as what Sarah offers, wouldn't you agree?"

"Are you suggesting that I should find a whoring maidservant?"

"Heavens, no," Kerry laughs. "Unless you feel that would be fitting to your current situation. No, James, I do believe that I could help you with beautiful Emma Hutchins."

"Help?"

"Of course," he says with a smile as he puts his tea cup down in its saucer once again. "I am willing to help you train her."

I swallow hard. "Are you suggesting that you take her to do your bidding as your servant has done moments ago?" My cock throbs as I recall the elegant oral copulation that Sarah performed upon her master.

"Women need some guidance when necessary, James. Emma is ready for such guidance."

"And how would you know such things?"

"The dinner party," he replies. "Did you not notice the way she responded to my presence? Or the manner in which I enticed her?"

"Enticed?" I had noticed the visual exchange between the two of them, but I would have hardly characterized what I saw as enticement. However, there was certainly a real connection between the pair.

"I am a businessman and a philanthropist, James. However, those parts of me are nothing compared to my ability to read a woman. Emma is ready for more than she admits to offering. She would have me bed her. I could see it in her eyes."

My cock throbs as it leaks into my trousers. To be truthful, I want to see my wife's legs spread as Kerry Thornton burrows into her small, wooly hole. If he could convince her to take his shaft into her mouth, that would be an added consolation. However, I doubt his abilities and I know that if I were to take him home to Emma it could lead to my own ruin.

"What would you do?" I ask. "If given an opportunity with her."

He smiles. "She will do as I ask, sir. Just as Sarah does for me now. It takes a little time with a woman in the bed to begin to change old stereotypes of sex." The word is rarely used in polite company in this way. Yes, *sex is sex,* but it's hardly so freely spoken about in the presence of those not involved in the marriage.

"Emma is a difficult woman to persuade of anything," I reply. "She won't go along so easily, Kerry."

"Aye, but she will," he tells me. "You only have to give me the opportunity, as you've noted. I swear that you will not be disappointed,

James. Bring me into her bed chamber and I will have your wife singing my praises." He smiles wickedly as my heart quickens its pace. What he speaks of is both dangerous and exciting. Were we to be caught by others, this scheme would end my career as a solicitor and my marriage to Emma. Though I usually eschew such risks, I can see where this could be a winning gamble.

"I'll arrange something," I tell him as my heart skips a beat. "It will have to be very lowkey. We cannot have others knowing what is going on."

"Of course." He smiles as he reaches for his tea cup again. I rise to my feet. "Leaving already?"

"Yes. I have some planning to do." I begin to walk toward the parlor door. "I'll see myself out. You will receive word soon of my plans."

"I'll look forward to hearing from you." Kerry raises his tea cup toward me and nods as I turn and walk out through the parlor door and then out of the manor house. The driver and buggy are still parked where I left them.

"It's time to go home," I tell the man. I then give him my address and sit back in the seat as we leave the small estate. What Mr. Thornton has said resonates in my mind as I consider Emma with him. Though I am a proper gentleman, there are needs that my wife rarely tends to for me. I want more. I need more. If he can help me get more from Emma, I welcome his help.

Chapter Nine: Giving Over

I've given Mr. Thornton's offer considerable thought over the last few days and finally he has been given my response. By way of delivery boy, I have sent him a note that invites him to our home tonight. Emma is unaware of my plans, and this fact makes me quite nervous. How she will react is anyone's guess. However, I have little doubt that she will become somewhat upset when she sees him darken our doorway.

"What is it?" Emma asks as she looks over at me from the small sofa where she holds her needlepoint in her lap. "You've been far too quiet, James."

I take in a slow breath as I put down my book. "I'm in thought," I reply. "There are some things on my mind at this time." Smiling at her, I ask, "Would you like to perform fellatio on me?"

Emma's eyes look questioningly at me. "What is *fellatio?*"

My cock becomes stiff as I begin to answer her. "It is when a woman puts her mouth on her man's hardness." I motion toward the bulge forming in the front of my trousers.

My wife gasps. "How vulgar! I thought we had moved past such things, sir." She's offended, just as I intended. If Kerry Thornton accepts my invitation, as I believe that he will, this will have her already ratcheted up quite nicely.

"I'm your husband," I say while chuckling. "Nothing is vulgar between us, madam."

"And I suppose you would have me bear my arse for you to take as well?" Her green eyes glare at me as her light brown hair sits just past her shoulders. I am thankful when my wife decides to take down her hair. It is alluring to me as I watch it move in the setting sunlight of the small parlor.

"Perhaps," I reply with a smile. This doesn't sit well with her as she puts down her needlepoint. Just as she's about to respond to me further, Carlton enters the room and interrupts us.

"Mr. and Mrs. Hutchins, there is a gentleman by the name of Mr. Thornton here to see you."

My body shivers as I reply, "Show him in, please." The butler nods his head and disappears for a moment.

"Kerry Thornton? Why would he be here, James?"

"I'm not certain," I lie. "Perhaps he will tell us." My heart races as the butler shows our guest into the parlor. "Close the door, please. No other visitors for now."

"As you wish, sir." Carlton closes the door and Kerry walks toward us.

"You are not welcome here, sir," Emma hisses as she looks harshly at the well-dressed man.

Kerry smiles. "It is my understanding that I have been invited." He turns his head to look at me.

"Indeed," I say as I get up from where I'm sitting. I walk over to a table where there is a bottle of sherry and partially fill a glass. "Welcome to our home." I hand the glass to Kerry and turn to Emma. She will undoubtedly have a tongue lashing ready for me.

"You?" Her eyes focus sharply upon me. "Why, James? What good can come of inviting such a cad into our home?"

"I believe Mr. Thornton would like to offer his apologies to you, my love."

"Oh, of course," he says after sipping the sherry. "I do apologize for the note, Mrs. Hutchins. I can see that it did not convey the message I had intended."

She frowns. "It seemed quite plain in its meaning."

"Aye, and I'm certain that it caused you great consternation, but if you would allow me, I do apologize now for the way it offended your pride."

"My *pride?* What about my status as a woman of society? I'm not some street whore, Mr. Thornton."

"No, that has been made quite clear by your husband in our conversations."

Emma narrows her eyes and looks at me. "What conversations, dear husband? What have you been discussing with this awful man?"

"Fellatio," I remark while chuckling. "You are a prudish woman, Emma. You won't do it and you won't allow me to even talk of such things with you. You're my *wife* dammit. You should be even more to me in the bed chamber than a whore could ever be. *You* should be my *whore."*

Emma is shocked and Kerry walks over to her as he unfastens his trousers. To the shock of my wife, he pulls out his large manhood and stands just in front of her. "Taste of this, Emma. I believe it is of excellent quality." He chuckles as he waves it before her.

"James," she stammers as she looks at me.

"You won't do it. He's just testing you and proving my point." I sit down in my seat after adjusting the wood inside my own trousers. "You might as well put it away, Kerry. Emma doesn't have what it takes to eat your snake."

Her face becomes red and angry as she looks at me. "You vile, vulgar man." She then turns and opens her mouth, pushing Kerry's rod into her throat.

"Madam," he gasps as she sucks hard on his cock.

"Fucking hell," I say as I am surprised by Emma's sudden act upon our guest.

"James," he grunts as he shakes his head. "She's bloody good at giving head." My wife reaches into his trousers and pulls out his ballocks so that she might fondle them with her hands. This is a side of my dear wife that I haven't seen before tonight. Emma never sucks on me, but what is happening now seems almost as if she has performed fellatio one someone before now.

"Utt..." My wife nearly vomits as she pulls him to the back of her throat, yet she continues to taste of the man before her.

"Stop!" Kerry pulls out of her mouth suddenly. "Emma, I'm very close." He breathes hard as he looks down at her. "I wish to defile your

sweet nether, my dear. Not your mouth. He helps my wife up from her seat and then pulls at her dress. Emma is wearing an evening dress, not the more formal type that she often wears when going out to see her friends. It doesn't take much for our guest to pull out her voluminous breasts and then to begin to suckle upon one of her nipples.

"Sir," she groans as Kerry pulls her large, pink areola into his mouth. My cock is hard and aching as I watch them together. Emma, though most often a prudish sort, is certainly no neophyte to what is happening in our parlor this evening. No, she has experienced the love of another man beyond our bed chamber. I'm curious as to where she has gained such an appreciation for sex.

Kerry pulls away from her and helps her remove her dress and undergarments to reveal her soft, curvy frame. Her bushy tuzzy muzzy is becoming wet from the quim she is producing. He picks her up and carries her to a card table nearby and lays her on it before pushing her legs back and forcing his face into her wooly beast.

"Oh, Kerry. Oh, *fuck."* The four-letter word, complained about by my lovely wife just days before, is now springing from her lips freely as she enjoys the way the man is rooting into her musky wetness. *"Fuck. Fuck."* She moves her hips around on the table as he puts his tongue into her. Kerry is a hungry man and he aims to satisfy said hunger by eating whatever nectar my wife might provide to him.

Kerry lifts his head and looks at Emma. "You are sweet as dew in the morning, my dear." He then stands up and removes his trousers and the rest of his clothing before pulling her closer to the edge of the table. His cock, solid and ready for her, slides into Emma's tight hole. She bucks a little as his ballocks find her arse crack.

"Ahhhh." Her body trembles at the feeling of Kerry's shaft deep inside her queefy cave. "Kerry. James." My wife looks over at me, her face red as she bites her lower lip. Emma enjoys the girthy manliness planted firmly inside her fertile furrow. *"Oh..."* Kerry begins to thrust into my wife hard, his skin slapping against hers as if he's beating her

with his hand. The sound and aroma of the vulgar sex they are having in our parlor causes me to spurt a little inside my trousers. I pull out my hardness and begin to stroke it slowly with my hand.

"Aye, you're a tight one," Kerry moans. He reaches down and caresses her breasts with one hand while keeping the other on her waist. "There are few who have such a fine feeling beaver, madam." He grits his teeth and adds, "Fucking cunt. Fucking little quim." He moves faster as he gets closer to seeding Emma's valley.

"My prudish love," I say as I pull up on my cock hard. A drop or two of clear fluid finds its way to the tip of my hard head and I run my hand over it. Though I can easily spill my own gravy upon the floor, I would prefer that a woman were here to catch it for me. Oh, that I could push my cock into Emma while the other man continues to fuck her so.

"Oh, this is so wrong," my wife moans in her thick Irish accent. "So very wrong. Vulgar and below my station...*ahhhh...*" Her body twists on the table as she suddenly climaxes with Kerry continuing to pump his pecker in and out of her. *"Ohhhh...OHHHHH!!!"* Emma squeals loudly and I worry for one moment as to what our servants might think of such sounds coming from the parlor. The butler and likely a maid servant will be nearby to be prepared to address our needs. However, they surely would know the sounds of intimacy and therefore keep to themselves as we enjoy ourselves in this room. *"Ohhhh!!! Fucking UHHHH!!!"* Emma strains on the table as Kerry begins to empty his ballocks into her.

"Oh, lassss...OHHHHH!!!" He pulls hard on my wife's legs as he forces his cock deeply into her moist muff. *"Mmmmm...uhhhh...ohhhh..."* His hips tense as streams of his white milk begin to fill her dark hole. Some of the seedy concoction begins to dribble from my wife's light brown hairs as she fills to overflowing. *"Emma. Fucking Emma."* Kerry breathes hard as he finishes pumping into her sweet cave.

"Uhhhh." A long, white stream of my manly milk erupts from the end of my cock and lands on the floor between my feet. *"Gawwww..."* I squeeze my rod tightly as I empty myself out all over the chair and the floor in front of me. Plenty of it finds its way onto my lap as well, causing me to grimace. This is certainly not the sort of thing I would have the maid come to clean up for me. *"Bloody fucking hell!"*

"Emma," Kerry Thornton says to my wife as he pulls out of her and steps back. His cock is now soft, but still long as it hangs before him. The man has successfully bedded my wife, even if it happened to be in our parlor on the top of a table.

My wife gets up from the table and looks at him and then at me. She finds her things quickly and pulls on her undergarments before walking out of the room through another door on the opposite side of the room from where Kerry had entered earlier. The door Emma has left through leads to another stairwell that goes directly to our bedroom upstairs.

"She says nothing," Kerry says to me. "I hope I have not offended beyond all hope for you, sir."

"Emma is likely surprised by her own response to you," I tell him. "She needs time to collect herself. Now she will have very little argument with me when I speak of our time together in bed." I smile. "I was surprised that she took to you as she did, Kerry."

He nods his head. "When I exposed myself to Emma, I thought she might scream or strike out at me. Honestly, I was concerned about your possible response as well."

"It was a bit of a shock," I admit. "However, she did take you into her mouth."

"She did." he replies with a wry smile. "James, she is a wild woman simply waiting to be untethered. It appears that she might be close."

"Close?"

Kerry nods his head again. "This is, for all intents and purposes, a one-off, James. Emma could go back to what she likes to do most, which is to be prudish and refuse to give in to your whims. You will need to strike while the iron is hot, so to say, if you are to keep dear Emma interested in such things."

"I see." I swallow hard as I look at the door where she exited. "My wife and I shall have a talk about what has happened."

"Please do." Kerry begins to put on his clothes as he adds, "If you need my services again, please do not hesitate to send word, James. I will be sure to clear my schedule if need be." I watch him get dressed and then walk to the door he came through earlier. The butler is there on the other side, a strange expression on his face, as he guides our guest toward the main door of the house. I realize that I still have my cock out, which must have been a sight to poor Carlton when the door opened. I quickly put it back inside and look for something to clean up the drizzled gravy on the floor, chair, and my trousers. If this had been spilled food or drink, I would have called for the maid. As it stands, I will need to attend directly to my own mess. I don't mind, though. I'm quite happy with what has happened between Kerry and Emma. That is all that matters.

Chapter Ten: Quite the Act

"Claira," I say to one of the housemaids working downstairs this morning. "Have you seen Mrs. Hutchins today?"

She shakes her head. "No, sir. Is she not still upstairs?"

"No," I reply as I look around the foyer of our home. "It's eight o'clock and she is normally still in the dressing closet at this time. She isn't upstairs." Though Emma has been known to occasionally rise before me, she typically waits for me before going downstairs for breakfast.

"Shall I ask the staff to search for her?" Claira asks.

"No, that won't be necessary," I answer. "She is likely somewhere else in the house. I'm sure she will turn up soon." I smile at the young woman as I make my way to the dining room. My mind thinks back to last night and what happened between Emma and Kerry. There was a connection of some sort between the two of them as they intimately gave in to each other. Excited about what I saw, I went to our bed chambers last night and found my wife already in bed. Though she wasn't as of yet asleep, we did draw close to each other and sleep very well.

"Good morning, Mr. Hutchins," the cook says as she stands near the dining room table. "Bacon, ham, and one poached egg," she announces. "Will you have any bread this morning, sir?"

"Aye, please." I sit down at the table and watch as she takes a decent portion of bread and put it on a separate plate before me. She then lays out different jellies and a large pat of fresh butter. "I don't suppose you have seen Mrs. Hutchins this morning, have you?" I look up at the old woman.

"She came through very early," the cook replies. "I was only just in the kitchen and she asked for something to take with her."

"Take with her?"

"Yes, sir. I gave Mrs. Hutchins some bread and salted ham. She took it in a small pail and left before sunrise. Surely she spoke to you before leaving?"

"No, she did not," I say as I grow concerned. "Have you any knowledge of where she has gone?"

"Not an iota," the cook answers. "However, she did leave in quite the hurry. I assumed it was urgent business with her charity or with a friend." She looks worriedly at me. "I do hope I didn't make a mistake by not asking her directly, sir."

"No, she probably wouldn't have told you anyway," I reply. I offer a slight smile to the cook and add, "She'll probably return home soon. Like you said, it's likely an issue with her soup kitchen charity or something equally important. Thank you." The cook bows her head and I watch her leave the dining room.

"Where have you gone, my love?" I ask under my breath as I begin to butter my bread. I no sooner take a bite of my breakfast that Carlton enters the dining room.

"Mr. Hutchins, this has just arrived for you by messenger boy." He hands me a sealed envelope and I look at it before opening it up. The writing is obviously that of my wife. I begin to read it in hopes that it will illuminate what has happened with her.

"Dearest Husband. I have gone to see someone that I have neglected to visit for the six years we have been wed. Please do not think ill of me when I tell you that this means that I have left Southampton for a time. I will return in due course, but you owe me patience and understanding after last night. My feelings concerning our marriage have begun to change, and I must put my thoughts to the test if I'm to be certain where we stand. Forgive my impetuousness in leaving without your prior knowledge or consent. I must do this. With love, Emma."

"What is this?" I say as the butler stands nearby. "Can she really be gone?"

"Gone, sir?" he says with some concern on his face.

"I don't know. She's gone, yet she says she will return in due time." Shaking my head, I ask, "Did the boy say where he was given this note?"

"No, Mr. Hutchins. He gave it over and left after I offered him a pence. The lad was quick on his feet as well."

"Alas, I wish I knew where my sweet Emma has gone." I'm concerned, as any faithful husband would be when his wife leaves without discussing it with him. Why would Emma leave? I fail to make sense of this turn of events.

"Would you like me to make inquiries, sir? I could contact other household staff in the area and see if Mrs. Hutchins has been in those homes."

I nod my head. "Please do, sir. Thank you." The butler nods and turns to leave the dining room. Alone, my mind begins to struggle with what my wife is up to.

"Where the bloody hell are you, Emma?" I ask myself as I sit back in my chair. "You know that you worry me so when you go without discussing first with me where you are going. Dammit, woman. *Dammit.*" I grit my teeth as I think about last night once again. The way Kerry pierced Emma's soft, wooly nethers continues to make me hard, even as I worry for her safety. Surely she has not gone to see him. No, her note says she has left Southampton altogether. Emma has gone somewhere that means something more to her.

"Dublin?" I question as my heart suddenly races. "That's where she's gone," I say to myself. "Back to Ireland. But, why? What is there that she needs to face now that she has had her time with another man? Is there a past man of mystery there for her? There is only one way to find out. "Claira," I call out. She's just inside the foyer and comes quickly to me.

"Sir?"

"Call for my horse and carriage, please. I'll be going to the train station."

"Yes, sir." She turns and does as I ask without question. Making my way back to my bed chambers, I begin to pack for the trip to Dublin. My only concern is that I have not as of yet told my soliciting partner that I will be leaving for Ireland. I will have to be certain to send him a message concerning my impromptu trip. The need to find Emma is overwhelming. She is my wife and I need to know that she's safe. Perfectly safe. No matter the cost, Emma is everything to me and I intend to get her back.

Hotwife Forbidden Adultery

Chapter One: Dublin

It has been some time since I last laid eyes upon the estate from whence my lovely Emma came to me. Far too long, I'm certain, if I were to have the opportunity to query my wife. She has missed her parents in the years since we two became one before a priest in Dublin. It was upon the insistence of her parents that it be so, and so it was. I, a ritualistically non practicing sort in the Church of England married a lovely young Catholic lass from Ireland. My father wasn't pleased about the arrangements, but then again he often scolded me for my decisions. I wonder what he would say now as the carriage that carries me comes to a stop before the door of the large manor.

"Sir," a young man smartly dressed says as he opens my door. I nod and step out onto the running board before taking another step onto the stone drive.

"Good morn, Mr. Hutchins," another man says in a thick Irish accent as he approaches me. "I trust ya travels were fair?"

"Quite fair," I reply while nodding my head and smiling. Clodagh is the butler of the house and English-trained if I recall correctly. Any house of high standing would require the services of a man trained in London. It has been years since I last laid eyes upon him.

"This way, sir." He turns and I follow him into the large house, the smell of fresh lilies wafting through my nose in the early morning breeze. Clodagh turns slightly as I follow him and says quietly, "The lady is not so pleased, sir. Mind yer tongue, aye?"

"Aye," I reply with a chuckle. Emma's mother, Margaret, is likely not very happy that I have come to see them without my wife upon my arm. I sent word just last evening of my arrival and received only a simple, terse response through the messenger boy that was likely full of expletives in Gaelic. When I asked him to translate, he simply smiled and walked away.

"Lady Collins," Clodagh says as he enters a large parlor and bows slightly. "Mr. Hutchins of Southampton to see you."

Margaret's back is to the both of us. She simply raises a hand and the butler again bows slightly before turning and facing me. He allows a slight smile before walking past me to the doorway, closing the door behind him as he leaves. Bumps arise along the back of my neck as I realize that I am alone with the lady of the house.

"James," she breathes out before she turns to look at me. "Where is my daughter?" Her steely blue eyes look hard at me.

I look away momentarily, her gaze sharp and painful. I've never much enjoyed being the object of Margaret's attention, even as I courted her daughter just six years earlier. Emma and I had met by chance, while she was with her father on a business trip in London. I fell for her immediately and I truly believed the feelings were utterly mutual, though at first my future wife would not admit as much. The only child of Mr. and Mrs. Collins, Emma was a precious jewel to them. One I quickly snatched up for myself, carrying her back to England where only letters between them could offer any solace for the loss.

"Margaret, I am searching for her as we speak. Emma came back to Dublin to see some friends, I believe."

"Friends?" The woman shakes her head. "And not her mother? I think not." Margaret is a beautiful woman. It would be foolish to say that some part of me would not want to slide into her as my cock becomes slightly engorged. Just sixteen years Emma's senior, the lady of the house still has the physique of a stunning creation.

"I assure you, Emma is safe and visiting her friends. I too had thought she might come by this way, but from your reaction, I can see this has not been the case."

"Not the case." Margaret's eyebrows raise. "And you have lost your wife."

"Not *lost,*" I immediately say to her. "I'm not certain..."

"You know that you have kept her away for far too long? Far too long for a young woman of her standing, James Hutchins."

I bite my lip. I'm sure the Collins consider me less than worthy of their daughter, but I am not without substantial holdings in my own right. Emma does not suffer for want whilst in my care. Anything she desires I will get for her, no matter the cost. Margaret walks past me, a hint of sweet aroma passing me as she makes her way to the couch. She sits down and puts her hands into her lap in a very ladylike manner. As she doesn't offer me the same option, I continue to stand nearby.

"You have kept her away from us." The accusation is again sharp, as I expected. "You are a shameful man."

"Shameful?" I shake my head. "Margaret, I can assure you, I am anything but shameful. Emma has lived a comfortable life with me. I care deeply for her."

"Do ya, now?" Her accent becomes a bit thicker for a moment. I am keenly aware that in this household Gaelic is often the language of choice. The Collins are a proud Irish family, which I cannot fault. However, their dislike for England is sometimes painfully apparent. My being English and not a member of the Catholic church, in particular, has been a difficult thing for Margaret to accept.

"Please, madam. Do you have any inkling as to her whereabouts? I would very much like to see her and offer her any aid she might require."

"Aid?" Her eyes flash at me again. "If I had such knowledge, do you honestly think that I would share it with you?" Margaret shakes her head. "Emma is likely better off without you, James. She has finally seen the mistake she made by putting her hand into yours. Go home and be glad that I don't have Clodagh come and throw you out."

The door to the parlor suddenly opens and a familiar face comes through the doorway. "Aye, what's this?" Dulon Collins walks in and looks at me and then at his wife. "Lad, I had no idea ya would be visitin' today." The older man smiles warmly and walks over to me. Taking my hand, my father-in-law shakes it while patting me on the shoulder with his other hand. "Margaret, when did he arrive?"

Margaret's eyes turn toward her husband. "He's not welcome here, Dulon. He's lost our daughter."

"I apologize, sir. Did you have no idea that I would arrive today?"

Dulon shakes his head. "Nary a thought, lad. Had ya sent word?" I suddenly realize that Margaret was the one who received my message the evening before. The reply must have also been of her creation.

"Yes, sir," I reply while nodding my head.

Dulon looks disappointedly at his wife before smiling back at me. "It's good to see ya here, James. Come, have a seat and let us speak of my daughter."

"Emma is lost, man. Have ya no care for her?"

Her husband chuckles. "Maggie, ya know where she be, aye? Why are ya so agin the lad?" Something is said by Margaret to her husband in Gaelic as she stands to her feet and walks quickly out of the parlor. From the look on his face, I can see that whatever his wife has said is not as pleasing as the floral aroma emanating from her body.

"I do apologize," I say as Dulon turns his attention back to me. "It was never my intention to unsettle your home in such a way."

"Not a thought, lad. Ye're welcome here, James. Always." He puts a hand on my shoulder and directs me to a chair nearby. I have a seat and wait for him to do the same. "So, my daughter has absconded?"

"She has," I reply. "Though, she left me a letter that explained she was coming to Dublin." I think for a moment about what happened before Emma's departure from Southampton. Her body, naked and beneath another man, his long sword piercing the velvet between her legs, causes my heart to beat rapidly for a moment. "I had believed that she would have come here first."

Dulon nods his head. "She sent word that she's in Dublin, but that she would come to see us in a few weeks' time. There is something she has busied herself with, lad." He smiles. "There is a streak of her mother in her. For that, I apologize to ya." We both laugh quietly as I nod my head. "Aye, a drink for yer lips?"

I nod my head and my father-in-law turns toward a small table between us. He picks up a small glass and fills it with a reddish-brown liquid from a flask on top. After handing it to me, he fills his own glass. We nod and have a sip before settling back to continue our conversation.

"Margaret has been hiding things from me, James. She has not forgiven me fer allowin' ya to wed our daughter." Dulon looks at the glass of whisky in his hand. "It would have behooved ya to have brought her to see us once each year, if at all possible."

I sigh. "I know, and I'm remorseful on that point. However, my duties in Southampton are numerous."

"The practice of Her Majesty's law?" He raises an eyebrow and smiles wryly. "Aye, I kin yer duties, James. Still, it has shaken Maggie to the bones to lay no eye upon the fruit of her womb. Letters alone can not salve wounds of the heart, lad." Dulon has always had a knack for words in the advice he has occasionally given me both before and after my marriage to Emma. It has been the sort of thing I have missed over the years since I took my wife back to Southampton with me.

"I have been dreadfully wrong," I reply. "Please, sir, forgive me." I nod my head toward him.

"Aye, lad. There's no need." He leans back in his chair while putting down his glass of whiskey on the table between us. Reaching into his pocket, Dulon pulls out a small scrap of paper and a tiny pencil. He puts the paper on his thigh and scribbles something upon it before folding it and handing it to me. "Maggie has told me where the lass might be staying."

I unfold the paper and look at it. "I will certainly look here for her," I reply. "Is she safe?"

"Safe? Do ya think her sire would sit so quietly here with you if Emma were in need of him?" Dulon raises an eyebrow. "James, she is your wife, aye? It is for you to go to her and bring her home."

"Of course," I reply as I slip the paper into one of my vest pockets. "I will do so, sir."

"After ya finish the drink, lad. Never waste a good drink." He reaches for his own glass and smiles before putting it to his lips and finishing it off. I do the same, the smooth yet fiery liquid sliding down my throat. Dulon comes from a working class of Irishmen, unlike his lovely wife. He worked his way up from selling coal by the brick or bucket to shipping loads of it to England and the European mainland. He is a self-made man of substance, but not once has he forgotten his roots. It is the likeliest explanation as to why I am here enjoying this whiskey instead of being on my head just outside the door of his large home. If Margaret had gotten her way, Clodagh would have boxed my ears and tossed me. Dulon is a man of principle. I have not yet and will not soon forget as much.

Chapter Two: Tenderfoot

I am forced to shake myself to relieve the nervous tension I feel inside as I approach the door of an unassuming home in the east of Dublin. The odor here is a bit off putting when compared to the entrancing aroma around Collins Estate. Lifting the metal rasp, I knock three times and step back to await the man or woman of the house. It is the latter who opens the door and peers out at me.

"Morning, sir," I say as I force a smile upon my face. "My name is James Hutchins and I'm looking for a young lady by the name of Mary Rose."

The tall, thin man looks from side to side along the dank street. His eyes, somewhat grey-blue and bloodshot, finally land upon me. "Englishman; here?"

"Yes," I say as I smile. "From Southampton. It is my hope that Mary Rose might have some knowledge as to the whereabouts of my wife, Emma Hutchins."

He reaches up to scratch through the scruff on his face. "Come in." The man turns and walks into his house and I follow, though with some apprehension. Unfortunately, the smells lingering in the air inside the home are a bit less of a delight as I close the door behind me. "Tea?" he asks as he rummages through a small pantry near the fireplace. "Nothing English, mind ya."

"Uh, no, but thank you for the offer," I reply. "I'm in quite the hurry, however. Do you know of a Mary Rose?" I look around the small home and note that although the odor inside is somewhat offensive, there appears to have been a femine touch to the abode at some point in the past. "I do apologize. What is your name?"

The Irishman reaches over to a small bucket of water and using a ladle scoops some into a small tin tea kettle. He then puts the kettle into the small fireplace where there are still a few embers left over from the evening. He turns to look at me as he runs his hand over his head.

"Name is Jacob Reilly," he replies before adding, "Mary Rose is not mine, but my wife's lass. I raised her as my own, though. Difficult one, that." He shakes his head as he makes his way to a small chair nearby. He nods toward another and I have a seat in the old wooden piece of furniture. "Things here are not as they were, Mr. Hutchins. Certainly not as I had hoped." He looks around the small living room. "The lady has left me and her daughter cares not to stay either."

"Your wife?"

The man winces a little before answering, "She blames the bottle, but I swore off it year last. I have no vices, sir. She just up and left."

"So, Mary Rose isn't here anymore?" Jacob shakes his head. "Oh." There is a deep sense of frustration within me as I consider the information my father-in-law gave me yesterday. I had hoped that it would have brought me to my wife immediately. Instead, I cannot find so much as her friend.

"Off with that tenderfoot," Jacob says with a growl.

"Tenderfoot?"

"The fool she off and went to," he replies. "That damned fool." He mutters something in Gaelic before getting up from his chair and walking over to the teapot. Though it has yet to make a sound, Jacob plucks it from the fire and pours some of the hot water into a cracked porcelain cup. He then lowers a small ball of tea leaves into the water before walking back over to his chair. "Are ya sure you would have none?" he looks at me and waits for a reply.

"No, but thank you," I answer. Jacob sits down with his own cup.

"Do you know where I might find her?" I ask. "My wife is likely with her. You see, they are friends."

The older man narrows his eyes in my direction. "Is she with that beast as well?"

"I...I don't know." I gulp as I think of the way Jacob is reacting to the thought of this other man. "Who is he?"

"Tagart McNally," he snorts before taking a quick sip of his tea. I realize that he has put no milk or sugar into his drink. Jacob appears to be content with the lack of ingredients, though.

"And where might I find Mr. McNally?"

"In hell, I hope," he replies with a gruff chuckle. Jacob takes another sip of his tea. "Elsewise, he's south of Dublin. A place called Kilteel, I believe." He puts his cup down and looks at me. "Are you going to kill him, sir?"

"Kill him?" My eyes grow wide until Jacob grins wryly.

"Aye, if ya would I would be very beholden to ya." He sits back in his chair and asks, "And what of Mary Rose? What are your plans with her?"

"None," I reply immediately. "I am only looking for my Emma, whom I believe to be with your daughter."

"My *wife's* daughter," he corrects me again. "The lass feels nary a thing for me, nor I for her. Other than that she has taken up with that tender-footed loon." Jacob snarls as he adds, "My good name is attached to her, Mr. Hutchins. I would kin that it not be spoken in civil conversation along with the name of McNally."

"I see," I reply as I nod my head. There is sense to be made of his distaste for the other man. If Mary Rose is indeed being bedded by the other man, she is likely to bring shame upon Mr. Reilly.

"Tell her to either marry that fool or to be off with him. My wife knew that she was a sore child in our lives together, and here she has gone off to hide herself from this shame." The man takes another quick drink of his tea before putting the cup onto the table nearby without a saucer. It would seem to explain why there are so many rings on the top of the old hickory tabletop.

"I'll convey your wishes," I tell him with a nod. "So, where is Kilteel again?"

"South of Dublin," he replies. "Tis' a village where her sort go sometimes. I've heard from others in the family that is where she makes her home..." Jacob's words seem to suddenly fall off as he considers what he's telling me. "The whore of a lass. A belting she deserves, aye?" He eyes me as he awaits my agreement. I nod my head as I get up from my seat.

"I should be off, then," I tell him. "No particular address, then?"

"You should check around the village, I'd guess. The inn there is where Tagart sometimes goes, or so I've been told told. If I had a few years given back to me, I'd go there and rap him terribly," the old Irishman tells me. "Go there and beat the lad for me, eh?"

"If I must," I reply. "But only if I must. It is my wife I am looking for, after all. Mary Rose will hopefully know where she can be found."

He nods his head as he gets up from his own chair. We walk to the door and he opens it for me. After I step outside, I turn to look back at Mr. Jacob Reilly. "May luck be with ya, Mr. Hutchins. It has not been so with me." The man then closes the door behind me and I turn toward the horse and small carriage waiting for me. The driver, a young man with a bright smile on his face, opens the door for me and waits for me to get inside.

"Do you know Kilteel?" I ask him as he looks over the side of the coach at me.

"Aye, I do, sir. Is that your next stop?"

"I am told there is an inn there?"

"Aye. Kilteel Inn. It's an old place and a tavern, sir. Lots of people visit." He shakes his head. "Not exactly a place for someone like you."

I smile at the lad. "If you can get me there, I will give you a bit more to make it worth your stay. Does that interest you?"

He nods his head and chuckles. "If you wish to visit Kilteel Inn, I will take you there, my lord. Any other stops along the way?"

"None," I reply. "Straight there."

He nods his head and tips his hat. "Aye. Straight there." The driver climbs back into his seat and lifts the reins before bringing them back down on the back of the one horse pulling the carriage. We are off to find Tagart McNally and hopefully Mary Rose and my wife. If not,

I will find myself right back at the beginning of my journey, without much to go on to find my beautiful young wife.

Chapter Three: No Tenderfoot

The Kilteel Inn has the smell of old wood and liquor wafting throughout as I walk toward the bar. A short and stocky man of about fifty years is serving another customer at one end as I have a seat at the other. I wait patiently for him as I look around the room. It's almost three o'clock in the afternoon and there are already patrons well on their way to softening the effects of the day.

"Aye, what ya for, sir?"

I turn to look at the barman. "A pint of ale, please."

He draws back and looks hard at me. "English, aye?" I'm not certain whether I am to answer the question or to take offense. The expression on his face is one of mild to moderate disapproval.

"English," I confirm. Surmising from his thick Irish accent, he must be taken aback by my differing accent.

"What's yer business, Englishman?" One eye in the old barman's head moves faster than the other and I wonder whether the slower of the two is damaged or even blind.

"No business of yours," I reply with a chuckle. "Although, I could use some information if you could please give me the ale that I've requested first." The barman snorts and allows an impish grin as he turns and picks up a large pint glass. After wiping it thoroughly with an old rag, he turns and fills it from a tapped wooden keg nearby. He then turns and puts the glass onto the table before me. "Thank you."

"I meant no bother, sir," he tells me as I take a quick drink from the glass. "Tisn't as if we see many of your kind here." The barman leans against the bar and looks at me. "What is it ya are here to ask me? It 'tis the true reason yer here, aye?"

After taking a quick breath, I reply, "I'm searching for a young man by the name of Tagart McNally. Have you heard of him?"

The short man raises an eyebrow. "Why would ya be lookin' for young Tag?"

"Business," I lie. "I need his help with something and I've been told by another that he's the one to speak to."

The barman laughs, snorting a little as he does. "Tagart McNally? You have business with the likes of him?" He shakes his head and looks into my eyes. "Ya don't look like the farmin' type, Englishman. Not at all." He looks around the room and adds, "There are loads of young men who come in here and would prefer not to be looked fer by the likes of an Englishman, sir."

"Farming type?" I've found myself quite caught upon the phrasing of this part of his response.

"Aye. Tag works the farms, sir. He's a hand fer hire. A boy with more cow shite on his shoes than most." The man leans over the counter. "No shite on yer shoes, eh?"

I have come to the thought that the barman is having a bit too much fun with me and I begin to get angry. "Have you seen him or haven't you? It is very important that I speak with him as soon as possible. Someone dear to me is missing and I think he might have seen her." I hope that something closer to the truth will loosen the man's tongue.

"A woman?" The smile erases from the barman's face. "Did he steal yer sister's virtue? Aye, the virtue of an Englishwoman." Though he doesn't smile, I can see that he's still quite pleased with himself as he leads me around and around in circles.

"Tagart might know someone who can help me, that's all," I reply while attempting to hold myself back from reaching across the counter and wringing his fat neck. "Please, can you help?" I pull out enough coins to pay for the ale in front of me and add to that enough to pay for a dozen more. Money at this point is no object to me. I need to find the young Irish lad I was told lived around here.

The barman's eyes open wide. "Aye, yer a bit serious, eh?"

"I am."

He nods his head. "Alright, then. Tag, or Tagart as ya call him, works for local farms when needed. He's a livestockman and a good one I'd wager."

"Not a tenderfoot?" I use the same term that was given to me by Mr. Reilly just this morning.

The short, stocky man laughs. *"Tenderfoot?* The man wrestles around with cows, goats, and sheep, sir. I doubt there's a tender foot on him." He continues to laugh before telling me, "Tag is a fine young lad and works harder than most. Sure, he has his faults, but nary more than any other man his age."

"So, where can I find him?" I push the coins in front of me toward him.

He takes a breath and answers, "I dunna know where he lays his head, sir, but he does come here most mornings for a hot meal. Tag enjoys sausages and eggs as well as the bacon we serve here. Ya might catch the lad here in the morn'."

I sigh. I had hoped for an address so that I could go right away to see this young man, but alas, I will have to find accommodations for the evening instead. Looking around, I ask, "Do you have rooms for letting here, sir?"

"Aye, but they're all taken." He nods his head toward the door. "Leave through that door and you will see a nice place across the street. The woman there has rooms for travelers." The barman straightens himself and adds, "Yer very serious about finding the lad, eh?"

"I am," I say as I look back at him and nod. "Can I trust you to not say anything to him about my needing to see him?"

Again, he raises an eyebrow. "I have no reason to, sir. Tag is no welp. He can fend for himself." The man looks at the glass in front of me. "Now, ya should drink that before it goes flat." He chuckles and moves away from me toward another customer along the bar. Lifting the glass of ale to my lips, I take another drink and think about what the barman has told me.

Tagart McNally is definitely not a tenderfoot as Jacob Reilly described him to me. It is likely that the offense the older Reilly feels toward Tagart for taking away Mary Rose is heightened by the fact that his wife left him after her daughter moved away. I can see how such a thing could bring a terrible flood of anger and rage out of a man, but to call a working man a tenderfoot or a leech upon society? It simply wasn't in keeping with civil conduct. I have nothing against the young McNally. Information is all I seek from him and I hope that he can provide something for me to use to find my dear Emma.

"Emma," I mutter quietly after swallowing the last of my pint of ale. Getting up from my seat, I make my way to the door of the tavern. Once I step outside, I can see across the street the establishment of which the barman spoke. After walking across, I enter the rowhouse and up to a small counter inside. A bell sits on top and I reach out to tap it so that it rings out throughout the house.

"Aye, I'm comin', says a female voice from around the corner. She walks around with an armload of bed linens and smiles at me. "Good day, sir. A room for ya?"

"Yes, a room please."

Her eyes flutter a little, the young woman smiling as they do. "English?"

"Yes, English," I say with a short laugh. The Irish are not often fond of my countrymen, but with good reason. However, I've found most that I've met to be at least lukewarm in their reception of me.

"You wish to stay more than a night?" I nod my head. "Aye, I can help you there." She smiles again as she puts down the bed linens and opens a large ledger-style book on top of the counter. "One room or will ya need more?"

"One," I reply. "It will only be me for now."

"Aye." A slight blush comes to her cheeks and I begin to think that maybe the young woman finds me at least somewhat attractive. This, of course, is gratifying, but something that I refuse to allow to distract me from the reason for my visit to Ireland in the first place.

"And when does the inn across the way serve breakfast in their tavern?" I forgot to ask the barman earlier.

"My guests can have a hot meal here, sir," she offers. "Only a small additional charge."

I nod my head. "I am to meet someone at the inn in the morning."

"Ah." The woman seems disappointed as she notates something in her book. "Seven o'clock, I believe." After turning the book around, she adds, "Please sign here if ya please." I take the small pencil from her and place my name on the line where she points her finger. The woman looks at the book for a moment. "Follow me," she says as she closes the book and slides it behind the counter. The woman turns and walks around the counter and I follow her. As we begin to climb a set of wooden stairs, she says to me, "My name is Annie. If ya need anythin', please let me know. My room is downstairs behind the counter." I follow the attractive young woman to a door on the second floor, one of three. She opens the door and waves me inside.

"Thank you," I say as I turn to look back at her. Her blue eyes are stunning in the light coming through the window of the small room.

"A bucket of water will be brought up each evening and morning. Clean towels are in the box at the end of the bed. Please let me know if ya will require anythin' more. Have a good stay, Mr. Hutchins." She allows one last smile before stepping back and closing the door behind her. I sit down on the bed for a moment as I consider the carriage driver who is waiting outside for me to secure a room and return for my things. He can wait a while longer since I am paying him so well.

"Emma, where have you gone? Why are you not with your parents?" These are the questions that have constantly bounced around in my mind since arriving in Dublin. I had expected to find my wife at the Collins estate, but alas, she was not there and her family had only a passing knowledge of her possible whereabouts. This distresses me a little as my mind again turns back to the driver waiting outside with my things. Opening the window in the room, I look down and call out to him. *"Driver!"* The young man, along with at least two others, looks up at me. "Bring my things and collect your payment, lad. You're finished with me."

"Aye, sir. Right away." He hops down from his carriage and reaches back for the two bags I have brought along with me. After closing the window, I turn to look around the room. Just a week ago, I was in Southampton enjoying what happened between my wife and another man. She had allowed him to plow her furrow deeply as I watched, and even now I am excited by the thought of it. My cock throbs for Emma as well as for the woman here known as Annie. I shake my head as I try to pass the thoughts away. My reasons for being here do not include indulging in another woman. No, I'm here to find my beloved wife as soon as possible.

Walking to the door, I open it so that I might begin the short journey downstairs to meet the carriage driver. There is so much that I have seen in the last two weeks that I feel as if I might burst. Emma and I have a great deal to discuss, and hopefully we shall do so very soon. Otherwise, I will be forced to return to England as well as to my solicitorship along with my cousin Phineas without knowing what has become of my wife. After all, a man has his responsibilities. The first among all, though, to his wife.

Chapter Four: A Tall Man

Seven o'clock in the morning comes early, yet I am up before the sun rises on the Irish landscape. I have spent the better part of the evening dreaming about Emma and the man she allowed to pierce her velvety nether. It was just after midnight when I felt compelled to relieve myself of some of the carnal angst I had been storing for some time. I can only hope that Annie does not realize what the dried residue on the bed linens happens to be when she changes my sheets later.

I have a seat inside the Kilteel Inn's tavern and wait for a young woman to make her way to my table. "Breakfast?" she says as she looks down at me.

"Yes, breakfast," I reply. "Eggs, toast, and beans," I say as I look around the room.

She nods her head. "English." It must truly be a different experience for some of the people here in Kilteel to hear my particular accent.

"Yes, English." I smile up at her but she does not return the nicety. The woman leaves my table and I sit back to watch the goings on in the room.

"A damned shame, that lot," I hear a man say nearby as he speaks to another man at his table. "Nary a one worth the spilled seed on his mother's bed." The two men laugh as they insult some nameless quarry. I find myself smiling a bit as I imagine the vulgar description, my own seed barely dry on the sheets across the street.

The door to the inn opens and a tall, dark-haired man walks in. "Tagart! Come here, lad." One of the men at the table nearby appears to know that man and call him by his name. This must be the Tagart McNally for whom I am looking.

"Good morn', ya old fool." They laugh and Tagart sits down at their table. "How are ya?"

"I'm doin' fine, lad. And you?" The older man pats the tall, young man on the arm.

"Ah, fine."

"There's work to be doin', then?" one of the other men ask.

"Always work to be doin', aye. More work that the two of you see in a month is what I do in a day." They all laugh again and I find myself chuckling as well. I want to get up and introduce myself to the young man, but then again I don't want to move too quickly. I'm not certain as to how he might react. Instead, I sit back and wait for my breakfast as he orders a plate of bacon and eggs for himself. Tagart McNally is a man of report in this tavern, I can assess as much from his way with the other men.

"The livestock blight in the county is spreadin', gents. More sheep are down 'er Kildare and further along." The young man shakes his head as a woman puts a plate of breakfast in front of him.

"Aye, the blight is a terrible one this year." An older man beside Tagart folds his arms across his chest as he leans back in his seat. "Likely more to come, as well."

"Sure, aye," another responds.

"And I'm puttin' down a dozen more this morn' fellas. Not fit farming for the lot of them right now." There's a sadness that forms on the young Mr. McNally's face. Whatever plague has struck the sheep of these parts, it's taking a toll on the county folk here. Even I begin to feel deeply vexed by their current plight.

"Yer a good man, lad. A good one, indeed." The older of the men pats Tagart's shoulder and they continue to eat and drink together. Perhaps this young man is an honorable soul and will give me aid as I seek my dear, sweet Emma. After all, any man who feels the wretchings of his common folk must have the sensibilities for the fairer sex to match.

They continue their breakfast as I continue mine, and at about a quarter hour before eight o'clock, they rise from their seats. My heart pounds within my chest as I also find myself backing my chair away from the table. Tagart and the other men lay down coins upon their table and after a brief wave, the young man exits the inn. I find myself doing the same and quickly walking to the door. Once I am outside,

I turn to my right to see Mr. McNally walking along the side of the cobblestone road. I follow, not exactly certain as to what I will say to him once I catch up.

"Do not make haste," I caution myself as I look around at the other people walking along. There is no need to cause anyone to suspect me of being someone of ill repute. Keeping my steps with those of the man of interest would likely cause others who are acquainted with him to question my reasons. Keeping back, I decide to simply follow him to his destination.

After no more than ten minutes, the young man enters a small pathway to the front door of an unassuming home. He walks inside and I am left to question myself as to why I did not try to make contact with him before he arrived.

"This is no farm," I comment as I look around. "I thought it would be a farm." I'm confused after overhearing the conversation between Tagart and the other two men. He spoke of killing sheep at a farm due to their illness, yet here he has come into a house in the east of the village. Why?

"Sir," I say to an older woman who happens to be walking along nearby. "Might I have a word?" She looks at me for a moment and scrunches her nose a bit as she comes toward me. Perhaps I have offended her as well with my English tongue?

"Aye?"

"Yes, well, do you know the occupants of this home?" I motion toward the small house.

She looks it over and then peers at me as her eyes narrow. "Why do ya need to know?"

After nervously clearing my throat, I reply, "I'm looking for a friend. I thought I saw Tagart McNally go inside? I tried to catch up to him, but his long legs make that task so very difficult." I present a lie to the older woman in hopes that she will accept it and yield some sort of helpful information. Of course, she could just as easily tell me to sod off.

"Yer an acquaintance of Tag, are ya?" she says with a raised eyebrow.

"I am," I reply. "He is supposed to do some work for me. On my farm." I honestly have no idea as to why I would say such a thing, but there you are. A terrible excuse to be given to someone who obviously knows the lad.

"In England?" she chortles. "A might distance for the lad, eh?"

I smile and attempt to keep myself steady. She has a keen mind, and she likely aims to uncover my true reasons for visiting here.

"Madam, I am in all honesty seeking my wife. I believe that Mr. McNally might know where I can find her."

She smiles wryly. "The lad does love the lasses." This doesn't help my state of mind as I watch her laugh again. "But, I doubt he can help ya. Tag is too busy a lad to meddle in the affairs of others."

"He knows Mary Rose," I reply. This name causes a change in her expression. The woman must know of her as well.

"Aye, Mary Rose. I have seen her around here as well. A good lass, if ever I have seen one."

"Without a doubt," I say as I try to reassure her of my intentions. "Please, madam. Can you tell me if Tagart lives here?"

She nods her head. "Aye, he does. Pays for a room, I believe. That's all I can tell ya, though. His personal affairs are his own, sir. Not those for others to meddle around in." I'm beginning to see that although she is willing to part with some information, she isn't about to share more than she feels comfortable sharing. There is a tightness within this village that should make any man or woman proud. If only such was the case in Southampton.

"And Mary Rose?"

The woman shakes her head. "As I told ya, he's a lad with his own mind. Nary a thought on my part as to his comin's and goin's." She then asks, "You seek your wife, aye? What has she to do with young Tag or Mary Rose?"

The question from her is an honest one. "Mary Rose and Emma are friends. They have known each other for a time."

"Ah. Do ya live here, sir?"

"No," I say as I shake my head. "In England with Emma, but my wife left and came here to see friends as well as her relations. Unfortunately, she did not leave me a complete itinerary for her visit."

"A lost wife in Ireland, eh?" She chuckles. "What have ya done to her?"

"Nothing at all, madam," I answer with a grain of stiff resolve over the slight insult. "We have a wonderful marriage. Emma is everything to me."

The woman sighs. "Embrace that while ya can," she tells me. "A good wife or husband is hard to find and keep. My own is an old codger with a sour disposition nowadays. One day he'll pass and I'll be free of his mouthings."

I don't know exactly how to reply to this commentary from the older Irish woman. It's apparent that there is little affection between her and the mister in her home. They have likely worn out any feelings they had in their marriage long ago, and that is precisely the fear I have when it comes to Emma. Certainly, the time she spent with another man as I watched seemed to be mutually enjoyable, but what if she has become ashamed or even outraged at my insistence that she do as much? Could it be possible that Emma has decided that I am no longer the mate she once desired? This fear has continually coursed through me as I search for her. If only I could see her so that we might speak on equal terms.

"There are others here, then?" I ask as I motion toward the small house. "Tagart rents here?"

"Aye, at least two others. I dunna bother in the personal affairs of others, sir. You should do the same." She nods at me and walks past me as she continues along her original pathway along the street. I watch her go and sigh as I consider what I know about Mr. McNally at this point.

"He's here," I say as I look back at the house. "And all I have to do is go and knock on the door." My heart beats hard as I think about what I will say and how I will say it. Tagart McNally is a tall, strapping man with the obvious ability to hold his own physically with man or beast. If I offend him in even the slightest way, I risk having my teeth knocked into my throat. I'm not here for any sort of physical confrontation, but I am an Englishman in a land that is tepid in its acceptance of me at best. Prying into someone's personal life in another land is not something I would have thought I would be doing just two weeks ago. However, I yearn for my dearest Emma more than I fear the man in the small home. So, I walk toward the door. As I step closer, I raise a hand to rap on the door. The fear inside me begins to boil violently as my stomach wretches with anticipation.

Chapter Five: A Surprised Woman

I knock on the door and take a deep breath as I await the person who will answer. As the door opens, small bumps arise along the back of my neck. A woman, not more than five feet in height, answers as she looks up at me. "Good morn'."

"Good morning," I reply. "My name is James Hutchins. I'm from Southampton in England and I am looking for my wife, Emma Hutchins."

The woman's green eyes grow wide. "Emma?" She looks back inside for a moment and then at me. "Come in, Mr. Hutchins." I walk inside the small house and she closes the door behind me. I look around the room and don't immediately see anyone else around.

"Tagart lives here?"

The woman looks over at me before opening a door. "Ya know him?" I shake my head as I decide to be honest this time around. "Could you come out here?" she says to someone in a room. I lick my lips nervously as I wonder whether she is summoning the man of the house to deal with me.

"James?!" Emma appears through the open doorway and shakes her head. "What are you doin' here, husband?"

"I should ask you the same," I reply as I feel my face flush red. I go to her and embrace my loving spouse. "I have missed you terribly, my dear."

"Aye, I've missed ya as well." Emma's Irish accent has thickened a bit since returning to Ireland just two weeks ago. "But, how did ya find me?"

I look at the other woman and then back at Emma. "Should we speak outside?" She nods her head and smiles at her hostess before we make our way to the door. After leaving the house, the door is closed behind us and we take a short walk into the yard.

"You were to stay home," Emma tells me. "I did'na mean for ya to come after me, James. I would have come home soon."

"But, when?" I ask. "You didn't even say farewell, my love. I would never leave you in such a manner as you left me. Never."

"Aye, I know. There are things that I needed to think upon for a while."

"About what happened between you and Thornton?" I say as I look into her eyes.

Emma nods her head. "It was something quite new for me, husband," she replies. "Quite new, indeed." Her face turns pink as she looks down at her feet for a moment. She then looks back up at me. "I've come to see what might have been with another."

I sigh as I look into her beautiful eyes. "The letter you left me said as much, Emma. But, why?" I have been confused since finding the letter from my dear wife early one morning. She stated that she was leaving for Dublin but there was little more than that other than she needed to find something out. "What are you looking for?"

Emma's face turns toward the small house as she replies, "I once held the love of another, but not in the carnal sense."

"Tagart," I say as I breathe out.

My wife looks back at me. "Oh, heavens no, husband," she replies. "Tagart is only a guest at this house, not a man who holds my interest."

"Mary Rose is his love, then?" She nods her head. "Then, of whom do you speak, my love?" I ask as I study the expression on Emma's face. I want to know. I *need* to know. After all, she is my wife. I willingly allowed her to be with another man before, but this is outside the bounds which I thought had been set between the two of us.

Emma sighs lightly and then takes my hand. "Ya must understand, James; Michael and I were together for a year before my father stopped my courtship with him. He didn't have the means to provide me a comfortable life, according to my father."

I haven't heard this before from my wife, so it causes me to become a bit uncomfortable as I look into her eyes. How could she have loved another before me? Certainly Dulon Collins would have never considered parting her from another man of Irish making? Would his financial capabilities really have put such a strain on the thought of welcoming a true Irishman into the family?

"Is this Michael here?" I ask as my voice quakes. Though I am trying to steady myself, I find that task to be very difficult. Sharing my wife's body with another man is one thing, but her heart is quite another.

"He's not here, no," she answers. "Michael is working today and his wife you just met."

"What?" I look at the door of the small house.

"Jenny. The woman who let ya in, James. She is my friend and Michael's wife."

"But..." I don't know what to say as my mind grapples with the information I am gathering from Emma. This Michael, a married man, is the object of my wife's affection? How could this be? How could Jenny allow such a thing?

"She knows," Emma tells me as if she can read my mind. "But she dunna know that I am so vexed by him still. This cannot be broached with her yet, James. Please promise me that much."

I shake my head. "You want for another husband, wife. How can I keep that to myself when his own woman is within the walls of that home?" My face turns red as I become a bit jealous. Though jealousy was present while Emma was being stuck in her muff by another man, my lustfulness far outpaced it. Now, however, she might have feelings beyond those of lust for another man.

"I have only just said something to Michael the evening before last. We are discussing our options."

"Options?" I glare at Emma as I grit my teeth tightly together. "Are you to break up our home and theirs?" It's a question I have had inside my mind since discovering that my wife yearns for a married man.

"No, my love. All I want for now is to see what could have been. I burn for him, James. I burn for Michael and I can't stand myself for it." She motions toward her flower with her hands as I look around. I quickly take her hands into mine before some civil folk along the street see where she is gesturing.

"You cannot be so obvious, my dear," I say as I look around. "What do you mean by saying that you are burning for him?"

"I am always wet, James," she answers as she looks down at herself. "I cannot stop thinking about him. All the time Michael is in my thoughts and I want to feel him inside me. I want to taste him and to have him taste me back."

"Oh, fuck," I say under my breath as I allow the vulgar word to slip through between my lips. There is no doubt in my mind that there would be a serious public discharge of some form of penalty for using such terms in the presence of a lady.

"Jenny, though, is not ready to know this." Her eyes dart away from me for a moment and to the small house nearby. "Michael thinks she will be willing, but we cannot know for certain."

"Shite," I say with another whisper. "You've gotten yourself tangled in a bit of a brier patch, woman."

"Aye, I have," Emma admits. "But I want to be here, James. Very much so." She then asks, "Would having Jenny beneath you make you happy?"

After swallowing hard I reply, "We should not be discussing such things out here in the presence of others, Emma." I look around and see about a half-dozen other people walking along the street. Though not particularly busy, there is ample food and carriage traffic past us that I feel such discussions are best had indoors. "Besides, you have only just informed me that she is unaware of you designs on her husband."

"I am aware," Emma tells me. After some thought, she adds, "Jenny is a very quiet lass, James. If she knew we were speaking of her..."

"You *are* speaking of her," I retort quietly. "This is very unseemly, wife. Very, very unseemly."

"So was allowing another man to shaft me, dear husband," Emma replies as she glares at me. "I ask only in return that ya give me due consideration."

"Michael," I say with a bit of seething breath.

"Aye. Michael."

I begin to pace back and forth in front of the small home as the morning sun lifts higher into the sky. There was no way that I could have predicted this day that my wife would make such a request of me. Had she made such comments to any other man, there's little doubt in my mind that there would have been severe repercussions for such. Even the looney house for her had she been so serious about such prospects. However, I am not the average gentleman. Emma is correct by reminding me of her encounter with another man. It was something that I wanted and she obliged, giving me the sort of lustful entertainment that few men will ever have the pleasure of experiencing.

"If this is to be entertained in thought," I begin, "It should be amicable all the way around, my love. If Jenny would not that we have this between us..."

"Then, you are at least willing?" Emma smiles as she looks into my eyes. I have apparently made the love of my life very happy.

"Perhaps," I say in return. "But this is very new to me, Emma. To have a woman other than you is not something I have considered before now."

"I know, and I love you for that," she replies. "Jenny would be happy to have you slide between her legs, my love. She will be ecstatic as you enjoy her around you." My wife is too certain of how the other wife will respond to the idea.

"Emma." I take her arm and guide my wife toward the front door of the house. "We cannot be caught speaking in such terms in public. There are laws."

"Aye, and you will keep us safe from them, right, husband?"

"This is Ireland," I remind her. "I am a solicitor only in England."

My wife giggles in a way that I have not seen before now. There is a playfulness in Mrs. Hutchins that is new and quite refreshing. Just now I realize that my manliness stiffens as I hold her close to me.

"You are aroused, sir," she says to me with a devious smile. "James..."

"Emma." I find myself gripped by the moment as I bend down and envelope her soft lips with my own as my trouser snake drips with lust. We kiss passionately for nearly a minute before I pull away and look up and down the street.

"Let us speak with her," she says to me softly. "Jenny is not as of yet convinced, but I would wager that she'll be moved by you and your needs, dear husband." Her eyes look into mine and I feel myself becoming even more aroused. There is something about the fairer sex that a man cannot resist. They have the innate capacity to control any aspect of their husbands' lives, either through wit or through lust.

"Alright," I say quietly. "Just know that I am not initiating this plan," I reply. "You are asking me to do this, correct?"

"I am," Emma says with a wry smile. "Jenny will enjoy you spreading her legs, my dear husband. You are going to give her something more to think about than her own husband."

I raise an eyebrow. "Her husband?"

"You will see very soon, my love." She grips my hand tightly and tugs at me until I follow her back to the house. Whatever Emma has planned, it will certainly be something more than I have considered within the confines of our marriage. Certainly, we took things a step out of bounds when my wife had carnal relations with another man in England as I watched the two of them together. That, at least for me, would have been the end of it all. However, it seems that Emma has decided that she has tasted the forbidden fruit and would now like to enjoy the entire platter. We shall soon see if this is to be the case.

Chapter Six: A Strained Relationship

"Jenny, could you get your husband?" Emma says to the other woman. Jenny looks from her to me before nodding her head and walking toward a door at the back of the house. She leaves and closes the door behind her.

"Where is she going?" I ask.

My wife keeps hold of my hand and squeezes it tightly. "Michael works in a shop just behind this house. They produce leather goods and other items." A door to our side suddenly opens and a tall man steps out. It's Tagart McNally. I take a quick breath as he looks at the two of us and nods his head.

"To work I go. I'm off." He nods his head again and leaves the house without so much as a greeting between the two of us.

"An odd man," I comment after the front door of the small home has closed.

"He's an *honorable* man," Jenny tells me without elaborating. Before I can ask anything more, the door at the back of the house opens and Jenny walks back in with a man behind her.

"Hello," he says to me as he walks past his wife and straight to me. The redheaded man is obviously a fit specimen of a human, his hand full of strength as he grips mine and shakes it. "I take it you have come to fetch yer wife?" He chuckles before turning to wink at Emma.

"Yes," I reply with a smile. "I'm James."

"Michael," he answers. "Though I would guess you already know as much, eh?"

"I do," I say as I look over at my wife.

"Then let us have a seat and enjoy a bit of tea." He looks over at Jenny and she quickly goes to fetch a pot of hot water. I watch the small, attractive woman move around the kitchen nearby as she prepares our hot drinks.

"I was just telling my husband that you and Jenny have allowed me time to stay here and think things through," Emma tells him as we wait for the other woman to join us. "I have been so grateful to the both of you for letting me spend time with you."

Michael nods his head. "We go back, don't we?" he replies with a softness in his voice as he looks affectionately at my wife. There is undoubtedly something between the two of them that would make most men jealous. For me, it brings about another wave of lustful feelings as I move around in my seat to allow my girthy meat more room to grow.

"We do," Emma admits as Jenny comes to the table with the teapot and four cups. She quietly pours us each some of the wonderful concoction before offering sugar and milk to add to them.

"Two," I say of the small sugar cubes she has in a dish. Jenny adds them to the cup before passing it to me. "Thank you."

Jenny finishes serving us before saying, "Emma is a good friend of us both."

"Aye, we've been thick for a long time," my wife concurs. "Like sisters."

After sipping at the warm tea in my cup, I ask, "Has Emma been catching you up with our lives in England, then?" This is my attempt to gauge exactly what has been said about the event between my wife and the other man. I would surmise that both Michael and Jenny are already well aware of our most recent history.

"We've spoken," Jenny admits. "About some things concerning yer marriage." She looks nervously at her husband and I can see that his eyes do not meet hers so easily. Whatever has been said, they are apparently not completely on the same page. This would seem to corroborate what Emma told me just moments ago.

Emma smiles after taking a drink of her own tea. "Jenny knows of the history I have with Michael," she begins. "She also knows that there is still some care on my part for her husband." The two women look momentarily at each other before Jenny looks away.

"Aye," Michael adds. "We have had our differences, to be sure. Differences that are a bit hard for the two of us." He swallows hard as his hands move around his cup of tea. "Jenny and I have nary been as husband and wife for going on a year."

"Husband," Jenny whispers over to him as she looks down at the table. There is embarrassment in her face as she blushes deeply. "This is not the sort of thing polite folk speak of."

"Polite?" Michael allows a short chuckle to escape his lips before he takes a sip of tea. There is an iciness between the two of them that is deep and painful, even for me as I sit quietly and listen to them.

"I have offered to do my duty to ya. Always I do," Jenny says. "Still, he's not the man I thought him to be. At least, not now," she tells us as she looks away from Michael.

"I'm a man, doh," he answers in his thick Irish tongue. "A man who deserves a woman who loves him more than this." Michael shakes his head and looks up at me, his blue eyes focusing upon me as if I'm a close friend or relation to him. "Not once did I lay a finger upon Emma, I swear to ya. Not once."

"He was always the gentleman," Emma concurs. "But, I turned him away."

Jenny shakes her head. "He wanted you and only accepted me as his only choice afterward. My life is cursed." She looks over at my wife. "Michael has moaned for you in the bed. Not for me."

My face turns red. Never before have I heard a married couple turn inward in such a way that they begin to spew every evil about each other to someone who until just minutes ago would have been a complete stranger. This experience continues to be painful for me as I hear how difficult things have been recently for the two of them.

"I wanted you, too," Michael tells his wife. "I have always wanted you, Jen."

"Aye, but only as a warm place for your thing, husband." She looks down and motions at his cock, "You've used me until yer tired of me, eh? Tired of my warm *faighean.*"

Michael scowls. "You have stopped coming to me, woman. I have done my part."

"Separate beds," Jenny says as she turns to look at me. "My husband will not bed me properly and will not be near me as he sleeps." Tears come to her eyes. "Can ya imagine such shame? They know. They all know."

"They?" Emma smiles lovingly at the other woman. "Who are they, my dear?"

Jenny presses her lips together as she looks over at Michael before turning back to my wife. "He tells his mother things. Very many things that are not the sort of things a wife would want told to her husband's mother."

"Leave her out of this," Michael says while picking up his tea cup. "She means you no harm, Jen."

"She wants you to find another, aye? She has no grandchild from me and my worth is naught."

"Wife."

"And you refuse to do what you must to give us a child," Jenny continues with anger in her eyes.

"Then other arrangements should be made," my wife interrupts. She apparently sees what I can plainly understand about the couple at the table seated with us. There is a rift that widens even now that will soon form a chasm that will be impossible to cross eventually. "Michael and I have spoken of such things recently."

Jenny's face turns red as she looks down at her hands in her lap. "I had thought you might," she says admits.

"You know what I want," Emma says as she looks at Michael. The two of them smile at each other for a moment before they break their gaze and the other man looks at me. He appears uncertain as to my current position on what my wife wants between the two of them. Even I am uncertain as to what I want as I think about what she said to me in the front yard not half an hour ago.

"I do," he says quietly. Michael turns to look at me and says, "I kin that ya would likely rake my teeth with your knuckles for saying as much."

For some reason, I smile and laugh briefly. "There would have been a time that I would have fiercely defended my wife's honor, but it appears that she is taken with you in a way that I cannot refuse." I've been honest at this point. Everyone at the table now understands that I am willing to allow my darling wife to take up with the young husband across the table from me. Even I am surprised by my quick acquiescence as I look over at Jenny. "There is but one thing that I feel might be a sticking point."

She blushes. "I have been faithful to but one man, sir," Jenny tells me. "One man for the last five years. I cannot be certain what my mind would have me do."

"You must think of yourself, Jen," Emma tells her. "This is what I have done to make my way back to Dublin and to find Michael. You must understand, I do not love him and he loves me not as well. This is nothing but a very physical thing, my sweet friend. Nothing more."

"Nothing more?" Jenny looks at her. "It is the breaking of sacred vows, Emma. I cannot do it. The Church..."

"Aye, the Church," Michael interrupts. "I give ya permission, Jen," he tells her. "It can only be a sin if you sin against me, aye? I give ya permission if ya give me permission, wife. Let us do what we both know we need to have done. It has been far too long."

Jenny's eyes water over. "But I love ya, Michael."

He softens a bit and puts his arm around her. "And I love you too, sweet Jenny. We still are who we are. We cannot divorce, but let us find some common ground." Michael then looks over at me. "I will let you have her to bed her for a time, but then I take her back, aye?"

I nod my head. "Aye." My heart beats hard inside my chest as I consider what I am offered. I have only ever enjoyed the warmth of Emma's loins before now. Sinking my cock into another woman has simply been a thought that would come and go from time to time inside my mind with passing fantasies. Never have I thought that I would have the opportunity to have my way with another woman. Especially not with one that is otherwise attached.

"Then it's settled," Emma says.

"Wait." Jenny shakes her head. "I need time to think on this. It is all just too much." She gets up from her seat and walks toward a doorway, disappearing through it before the door closes behind her.

Michaels sighs. "Jenny wants this as do I. I can see it in her manners even now. She will come to see it this way eventually." He looks at me again. "She is the gentle sort in bed."

I nod my understanding before Emma says, "We will go. Michael, you and Jen will speak on this while I take James on a walk. We will return later for your answer."

"I will." We all stand and I shake Michael's hand before Emma embraces him and kisses him on the cheek. There is a small bit of jealousy on my part, but nothing so severe as to want to strike him. No, I am quite excited by what has been discussed here. It will take some time for the young woman of the house to consider it all, though.

As we walk out the door, I ask my wife, "Why here and why now? Why not years ago?"

Emma sighs. "When I did what I did a few weeks ago, something changed inside me, James. Something quite monumental." She smiles at me and takes my hand as we walk along the street. Where we are going, I have no idea. I go along with my dear wife to see what she has in mind. I'm certain it will be an adventure in and of itself.

Chapter Seven: An Uncommon Approach

"What you have asked of all of us is uncommon, my love," I tell Emma as we walk near a small stream on the edge of the village. "If any were to discover this plot, we would all be completely undone."

"Aye, we would," Emma admits as she stands beside me and watches waterfowl such as ducks and a few geese nearby. "Yet, it is done, James. Quietly, to be sure."

"Quietly." I shake my head. It is true that I want Jenny carnally just as Michael wants my wife to bed. However, there are laws and societal understandings that must be given at least some consideration. If we are found out, we risk being thrown into prison for adultery. Though I consider myself to be a skilled solicitor, there is little I could reasonably do to counter such charges if they are found by a judge to have merit. No, we are finding ourselves out on a narrow branch with wild boars just below waiting to devour us. Allowing Emma some time with another man is one thing, but actively swapping our partners is another, more dangerous thing entirely.

"I understand yer concern," my wife says in her thick accent. It's amazing how quickly she has traded in her anglicized speech from where she has lived the last few years. "But nary one will go to the authorities."

"Perhaps not," I say while nodding my head. "Jenny, however, is not completely of the same mind, my love. We cannot push her into something that she does not want."

"James, she is keen on the idea," Emma counters. "Jen needs a little time to consider her position, that's all." My wife puts her hand into mine. "They have had a very dry union for the last year, and we might be able to help with that."

I take a breath and ask something I have been thinking about for the last hour or so. "Were you corresponding with Michael before you came here?"

At first, my wife says nothing. Instead, she simply stares out at the water in the little stream. My heart strikes hard as I consider what her immediate nonresponse could mean.

"There were two letters," she admits. "To Jenny, but then Michael wrote back once. I didn't intend to come here, James. At least, not when I first spoke to them. My plans changed to come here and see the two of them before coming back home to you."

"You left in a terrible way," I say as I feel anger rise up within me for a moment. There has been absolutely no rage in me toward my dear wife up until this point, but instead I have felt as if she somehow wronged me by leaving without so much as a real explanation. A note is all Emma left me, and even with that a somewhat vague reference to Dublin. She could have done better, to be certain. I suppose there is a part of me that would like some sort of apology over how she handled leaving our home.

"I'm very sorry," Emma says as she turns to look into my eyes. "I didn't know what to do at the time, James. The need to leave just...overtook me."

"And you came to see an old beau." I bite my lip for a moment before adding, "That doesn't look proper, my dear."

"Aye, not proper at all," she agrees. "I am very sorry. Please forgive me for not thinking more about you, James." Emma bends forward and kisses me on the cheek. She loves me and I love her as well. If only we could have spoken before she left we might have come to some understanding as to what she would be doing.

"This idea," I say as I shake my head. "That you would like to be with Michael and that I would be with his wife. It's a difficult thing to do, Emma. There are laws..."

"You have said as much before, James, but there are many who do not heed them at times, aye?" Her eyes stare hard into mine. "We shall be discrete, husband. We will not be the first to do such a thing."

"No, not the first," I agree. "However, my standing in Southampton would be ruined if we were found out."

"And mine?" she retorts. "Am I not within the same society?"

"My vocation, Emma. My practice as a solicitor would be ground under by the order of a high magistrate if I dishonored myself. We must be assured of absolute discretion if we are to take part in anything with those two."

My wife smiles wickedly. "Admit that ya would like to fuck her, love. You would like to fuck the fair Jenny." There is a stirring within my trousers as I turn to look back at the water. Of course I would like to feel the young woman's soft cunt around my swollen timber. No man after having looked upon her could say otherwise. That does not remove the fact that I would be taking a tremendous risk in doing so.

"Emma, we are in public," I say as I look around. Deciding to change the subject, I continue, "What of Mary Rose? Her father was quite certain that she was taking up with that Tagart fellow."

My wife sighs. "They are in love," she replies. "Though, they have been pure with each other. Mary lives in a small home nearby with an elderly couple. She cooks and keeps their livestock and they provide a place for her to stay. It has been a comfortable arrangement for her."

"And the man?"

"Aye, a good one. Strong, but gentle. He's been kind and generous to Mary Rose since they met. I've no doubt that they will wed soon."

"I see." I nod my head as I consider what Emma is telling me. "And you have not spread your legs for him? Not once?"

She turns and looks at me, her eyes glaring as she shakes her head. "How can ya dare to say as much?" Emma purses her lips together before continuing, "Do ya have such little faith in me as to make such a terrible accusation, husband?"

"I apologize, my love, but he's a strapping lad and I thought..."

"Men," she seethes before turning and looking across the old road.

Turning, I put my arm around Emma and smile at her. "I am a cruel man at times, my love. You know this to be true. 'Tis not the way I should have approached the question."

"There should be no question at all, husband." Emma pulls away, obviously hurt by my vile remarks. How could I have been so caddish?

"My apologies again, madam." I bow to her slightly as she turns to look at me. "Please accept a terrible husband's apology. I cannot live without you."

"James." She walks back to me and puts a hand on the side of my face. "I didna come here to spread my legs for just any man. You will always know my desires, sweet one." We lean toward each other and kiss for a few moments, her soft lips gripping and enveloping mine as my beastly cock throbs for her as well as for the other Irish wife. My loins are full of the white soup that I so desperately wish to leave deep inside Jenny's tender kitten. Oh, how I do crave her!

Emma pulls back and says to me, "James, we will need to convince Jenny to allow us to enter their bed."

After swallowing hard, I ask, "Is there any sign as of yet of her willingness to do as much?"

My wife nods her head. "Aye, she did seem softened to the idea when Michael mentioned it a while ago, but not so much as that she is ready to move forward. We will need to speak with her as well as with Michael. Their marriage has been rough for some time."

"Rough?"

"Nary a warm night for Michael's cock," Emma says directly. I rarely hear such language from my wife, but it no longer surprises me as I am still considering her question to me only minutes earlier.

"Are they without marital relations completely?" She nods her head. "I see." My heart pumps hard within my chest as I consider how the two of them must be burning with desire. It would be a fine thing if I were to pierce Jenny's soft velvet after the absence of Michael's pole inside her.

"For nigh on a year, husband, they have been without. Michael tells me that his loins have burned with desire. He craves me, James. 'Tis why he answered me after I wrote to Jenny."

"I crave the young woman as well," I admit to her. "Very much so."

Emma reaches toward my large bulge in the front of my trousers and smiles. "I can see that, dear husband. You do seem to have the need to do something with this before it falls off." She giggles for a moment as my face burns with redness. My wife has always had a way of enticing me in such ways. I love her for it and wish for the both of us to get what we truly desire.

"Then what shall we do?" I ask.

"We shall speak to them as friends," she replies. "Calmly and without fear. However, I will need time to prepare Jenny. She is far too prudish at this stage. I will help her to step out a bit and perhaps we shall be able to get her to bend to this new idea."

"A new idea." I chuckle. "If only Phineas were here to know of this."

"No," Emma says forcefully. "Leave him out of this, James. Your cousin would share too much with others and ya know it. Not a word of this to him or to anyone else. You have said as much yourself that this is dangerous."

"It 'tis," I say with a nod. "Then you will do your part and I will go back to my current accomodations and consider what you have said. Would that suit you, my love?" I reach out and run the back of my hand along my wife's soft face.

"Aye, that would be fine. I love ya, husband." She leans in and we kiss once more before Emma turns and begins to walk back in the direction of the small home where Michael and Jenny live. I turn and begin to walk back to where I have taken out a room for a time.

"James, this is without a doubt a much different path than laid out in your marital vows," I tell myself as I walk slowly along the road toward the house where I am staying. Emma's predisposition to take up like this with another man is somewhat surprising, though it is not the first time. What is even more startling for me is that she appears to want me to spread Jenny's legs to my own satisfaction. Having a wife say as much undoubtedly is a rare thing. Something has been aroused within my love for such things, likely due to the time she spent bedding another man as I watched. Even now, my cock hardens as I think of him pushing his manly form deep into her wet cavern. If I had the option now, I would pull out my own cock and tug at it until I dropped my seed upon the ground. As it is, there is not one spot along this street where such a thing could be done away from prying eyes. This is a task that will be best suited inside the room I have let from the owner of the house. She seemed keen on me when I came into her home as well. Perhaps there is something there I should investigate? I shake my head and laugh to myself as my completely solid male ego below continues to throb. No, that would not be proper. Though Emma and I have decided to move forward in our lustful new life, I will continue to be faithful to her. That is, I will only fuck whomever she allows me to fuck.

Chapter Eight: An Elder's Experience

I nod my head toward the young woman after she brings me eggs, beans, and toast for breakfast. As she walks away, I notice someone coming toward my small table. An older man, smelling of some common occupation, has a seat next to me.

"Aye, a fine meal that is." He smiles, his mouth lacking all but three of his teeth.

"Sir?" I look him over as I shake my head. "There is plenty of space there and there." I nod toward the other tables nearby.

"Aye, sure, but I dunna like to eat alone." He waves the woman from earlier over and says, "A bit of the porridge, if ya dunna mind." The woman nods her head and leaves.

"I'm sorry, but you will need to kindly..."

"Rupert Longfellow. Brought forth in England, raised in Ireland, and soon to be buried here as well." He chuckles as his old grey eyes look me over. What is left of his hair is tossed and long, a sign that a pair of shears have not seen his head in several years.

"You're an Englishman?"

"Aye, I was. Mother brought me here when I was but a small lad. Father had passed and her family was here." He smiles at me. "Eighty years I've been on this Earth, and likely I'll be leavin' soon." The woman appears with his bowl of porridge and he thanks her before picking up the spoon and shoveling a large amount of it into his mouth. Rupert is likely avoiding the same sort of meal that I am consuming due to his lack of teeth.

"And why are you here? At my table, that is?"

He smiles. "I heard yer accent, lad. Thought it would be nice to see another from my old homeland."

"Ah." I look around and can see that there are others staring at us. I'm certain they have dealt with old Rupert in some way before. "What is it that you do, sir?"

"Coppersmith," he replies after allowing the porridge to slide down his throat, his Adam's apple bobbing up and down as he does.

"Sixty-two years I've been at it. The best in the land." Rupert winks at me. "Likely that's what ya smell, sir." He's noticed that I've put my fingers to my nose multiple times since he sat down beside me. I cannot help but wonder whether it's the products of his smithing occupation that offend my senses, or the fact that he's likely not been bathed in weeks or even months.

"That explains it," I say as I feign agreement.

"What are ya here for?" he asks just before shoveling another bite of porridge into his mouth.

"My wife," I tell him, though I know I shouldn't. "She came here and I am here to fetch her back."

"Yer wife? Did she leave ya?"

"No," I say as I shake my head. I'm offended, but can see why he might think as much. "She came to see family. That's all."

"Ah. No wife fer me, sir. No, not a one. They are too much the bother, they are." He takes another bite of his meal before wagging his spoon in the air. "But a woman. I can have one when I want, aye? That for sure isn't the problem." He chuckles, nearly choking on the food he has just put into his mouth. I merely smile as I look back at him.

"A woman? Do you have one somewhere?" I ask with a smile.

"For bedding? Aye, I bed a few around here," he replies as if he is serious. As I study his expression, I get the feeling that he is indeed very serious. Leaning toward me, he adds, "A tugging I need occasionally when the old goat downstairs is with horn." He laughs before looking around the room.

"Where?" I ask. "A brothel?"

He smiles. "Brothels, taverns, and the like. Dunna be deceived by my clothing, sir. I have money, and lots to be sure." Rupert winks as he sits back in his chair. He has finished his bowl of porridge rather quickly in just a few large bites. "Are ya inclined for a poke with a lass, sir?"

"Uh, no, but thank you." I reply as my cheeks become red. "I've a wife, as I've said before.

"Yes, but a poke is a poke, isn't it? The misses dare not need to know." There is a gleam in his eyes as he looks at me steadily. He likely knows that I am but a fly in his web at this point. I'm unable to wriggle free of this conversation without leaving my breakfast behind.

"My wife would understand, actually," I say without completely grasping why I would say such a thing to a stranger. "We have an understanding between us."

The old coppersmith's eyes widen. "So, yer one of those, eh?" He smiles. "I wouldna mind a wife if she could agree to such a thing. To be able to grease the old pecker inside another woman once in a while is all that I would need. 'Tis a rare thing, sir." He nods his head at me as he continues to smile.

"We must agree," I continue, "Or it does not happen."

He raises an eyebrow. "Have ya done another while she watched?"

"No," I say as I look around. I worry that someone else might hear and understand our conversation. "She has been with another as I watched, but not the other way around."

"Aye. A fantastic thing, to see a woman with another. I have on many occasions, lad. Many occasions, indeed."

"Seriously?"

"Aye. Women with women as well. 'Tis a thing of beauty when two fillies are buckin' in the bed." He allows a laugh as he folds his old, wrinkled hands on the table before him. "When they taste of each other, it causes my old goat to rise. Have ya had the pleasure, sir?"

"Two women?" He nods his head. "No, I have not."

"Then ya must try to get the misses to do that for ya, sir. Have her lay with another woman."

My heart races inside my chest as my cock becomes hard. The thought of Emma with other men has been a constant lustful fantasy of mine, but not once have I considered her with other women. To think of it now seems naughtier than my previous ideas. Would my wife consider such a thing at all? Perhaps with Jenny? Or even with another woman?

"Have ya shared her with another man? And then you a wife of his?"

"No," I reply as I come back from my daydream. "Not yet."

"Ah, but ya are thinking about it?" He smiles. I do not have to answer him directly. Rupert seems to already know where my thoughts lie.

I swallow hard as I collect my thoughts. "We have discussed it. There might be some opportunity, but I'm not certain if it will work out."

"Give it a toss, eh? You'll both be happy that ya did."

"Right." Why am I speaking with this coppersmith at all? He smells and it's obvious that he has a mind full of debauchery and other wicked things. Were I a man of integrity, I would rise from this table and declare to the entire tavern that Rupert is a man of ill will and that he should be confined as such. The damned old man is full of wild fantasies that he has begun to impart to me. Why do I allow him such leeway? What has become of me and my moral standing?

"Well, lad, I have much to do today. A long list of orders await me and I must fill 'em." He gets up from his chair and walks out of the tavern as quickly as he entered in. His empty bowl sits on the table near me and I look into it as I consider all that has been said between us.

"There is something to his words," I tell myself, though I don't want to believe my own. "The old man is onto something. I love Emma, and I'm damned glad that we are married, but there is so much more. We've already experienced that together." I think about the conversation I had with my wife yesterday afternoon before I returned to the boarding house. Emma is ready to have Michael spread her legs and she's happy to allow me to do the same with the man's wife. All it will take is to convince Jenny of going along with our plan. Though I have no idea what I can do or say to facilitate this act, I could see that my wife is committed to do as much. Jenny trusts her and I think that there is some merit to the thought she has put into it. What will Michael think to have me as his wife's lover?

"Sir, will you be paying for his porridge?" I look up to see the young woman standing nearby.

"What?"

"His porridge. Rupert has gone and he was your guest, aye?"

I swallow hard as I look down at the empty bowl. "That sly devil." My eyes turn back to the woman. "I'll pay for it," I tell her. She smiles as she reaches down to retrieve the empty bowl as well as my plate. The old coppersmith has gotten his breakfast for free, but I have likely gotten a valuable conversation in return. Before speaking to him, I did not consider the idea of having Emma eat another woman's velvety kitty. No, such a thought had never really crossed my mind. Now, as I sit here and consider this possibility, I am hard and throbbing with excitement. Perhaps there could be an understanding between myself and sweet Emma that will be agreeable to her? Perhaps my wife would consider as much when we go to see Michael and Jenny today? We shall see.

Chapter Nine: Giving In

There is an awkward silence in the unassuming home as I sit quietly beside Emma. She has spoken for the last few minutes on the positives to be had were the four of us to give in to our more primal urges and fuck each other. Michael, though moved at some point to agree with my wife, seems concerned for the expression on Jenny's face.

"It changes nothing," he tells her. "Except that we have not had relations in so long, Jen."

Her face scrunches a little as she frowns. "You want her so badly, aye?" Michael slowly nods his head. "Then you have already made up your mind." Jenny's green eyes focus hard on her husband as he looks away. Their marriage bed has been cold for at least a year according to what I have gathered from the information given to me by Emma. This alone seems to be driving the young Irishman toward wanting my wife. Well, that and possibly the fact that the two of them share a history from before that was not fraught with such a close and carnal relationship.

"Perhaps this is a bit much for you both," I offer as I look over at my wife. "My love, certainly you can see that there is a great vexing here between Michael and Jenny. We should remove ourselves and allow them to mend their bond."

"No, I think that Jenny is playing this up a bit, husband."

"What?" Jenny looks at her old friend as her mouth drops open a little.

"You know of what I speak, aye? Jen, you and your husband have had nothing together for so long. You both need this so that you can move on with each other."

"Give ya my husband, eh?" Jenny shakes her head as she glares at Emma. "That would suit ya?"

"Aye, suit me fine. But only for today. You can have 'em for the rest of your life, Jen."

"Ladies, we should do as James suggested," Michael chimes in. "Perhaps some separation..."

"Nay, no separation," Jenny replies. "We'll have this out now. You have had a burning for him this whole time, Emma. Tell me 'tis not the truth."

My wife smiles wickedly. "Aye, I'll not lie. I have wanted Michael for a time. To feel his naked body agin mine would be somethin' of great value to me." Emma then looks over at me and continues, "My husband would do for ya the same, Jen. It would be a fair trade."

"Fair?" Jenny looks at me. "How so?"

"Ladies," I interrupt again. "Please, let us separate and give some time for whatever wounds are here to heal. We do not need to push things any farther if there is not a common agreement. Emma, you know that you and I have had such an agreement between us. Michael and Jenny clearly do not."

"No, we appear to not have any agreement," he replies. "My wife is quick to anger and to accuse, but slow to allow me to warm her sheets. Not one time in the last many months have I seen ya naked, Jenny. It has been too long and my loins do burn for someone...anyone."

"For a former sweetheart, eh?" Jenny's eyes fill with a few tears. "You care not for me, Michael? I am yer wife."'

"You are, aye. That will'na change either. We are bound tightly. I am a man of my word." He smiles at her and asks, "Can Emma at least give me some pleasure, even if not in the fullest sense?"

Jenny looks from her husband toward my wife and then to me before looking once again at her husband. "What would ya have?"

Michael looks to Emma and my wife speaks. "Let me show you, Jen." She gets up from where she is sitting and goes to the chair where Michael is sitting. He stands to his feet and my wife goes to her knees. She opens his trousers and moves her fingers inside to find his fleshy, hardening phallus. Emma's lips part and allow his hardness to move into her mouth.

"Emma," he moans as he feels my wife's full lips around his cock. I become a bit hard as I watch her enjoy the other man's long pole inside

her mouth. Jenny, surprised by what she is seeing, turns for a moment and looks at me."

"James," she says to me. "She is your wife. Do ya have no worry 'bout this?" I watch Emma move her lips along his long stalk. My wife pulls out his ballocks and begins to finger them as he puts his hands on top of her head.

"Nary a concern," I answer the young wife. "Emma knows what she is doing. Michael appears to need what she offers." I watch with intense interest as the two of them move around, his cock slowly moving in and out of her mouth with my wife's head bobbing forward and back. They seem almost as if they have been married for a time and this is completely natural for them.

"'Tis a sin," Jenny remarks. "To do this at all, 'tis a sin."

"'Tis not a sin," Michael moans. "You have refused me this one thing, wife. Your mouth..." He moans again as he closes his eyes and allows Emma to suck his large cock.

"Do you not do this for him?" I ask Jenny as I move my swelling member around inside my trousers.

She shakes her head. "Never. It is considered a sin in the Church to do such a thing. The nuns have spoken of such and said there is only one place to put a man's thing. 'Tis wrong to put it inside the mouth."

"Have you done as much before?" I ask as I feel the tip of my cock become a bit wet. I would welcome wholeheartedly Jenny's sweet, full lips on my own shaft.

"No," she answers quietly. "The taste..."

"Try mine," I say to her. I pull my own swollen manhood from my trousers and hold it in my hand. Moving my hand up and down, I caress it as I dribble a bit of clear liquid from the end. Jenny's eyes grow as she looks upon me.

"Sir, this cannot be." She turns to face away from me.

"Have I offended you?" I ask as my own face turns red.

"I'm married, sir. And you belong to another."

"Another that is sampling your own man's cock," I remind her. Jenny looks back at me and her eyes lock onto mine. She then looks down at my hardness and reaches slowly toward it. "You can hold it," I say to her. "Pull on it for a bit if you please." My body bucks a little as Jenny's small, soft, warm hand envelops my cock.

"'Tis large," she tells me as she slowly moves her hand up the length of my hard pole. "Very large." Michael's wife blushes as she continues to feel of my girthy manhood. He cares not what Jenny does as Emma services him nearby.

"Kiss it," I plead with her. "Put your lips to the tip of it, Jenny."

"But, sir." She looks at me, her green eyes studying me carefully. I would have to guess that she would like to do as I ask, but that she still worries what the Church might think of such a thing. Even so, they will never have to know. I would never share such a secret.

Jenny bends down a little and inhales the aroma lightly from my nethers. I have bathed, so I am confident that I will not offend. However, it does bring some redness to my cheeks as I consider how cautiously the young woman approaches my organ. Of course, it is imperative that I remember that she is very new to such things. Jenny has not licked or suckled a man's cock before. Not even her own husband's.

The young woman kisses the end of my cock lightly and I buck a little. "Jenny, your lips are soft," I moan at her. Michael opens his eyes to look over and see his wife applying a second kiss to the tip of my manhood. He smiles.

"Do you really like this?" she whispers to me.

"Yes, my dear. I like it and would like whatever you will give me, Jenny. Do what you please." I sit back in my seat and watch Jenny continue to kiss along the length of my stalk, her lips making their way along the warm skin. She takes her time to explore all of me before allowing the head of my cock to enter her mouth. I feel myself ooze a little onto her tongue, causing her to suddenly rear back from me.

"Oh...oh, no." Her eyes go to me as she wipes her lips. "Did you put your seed inside my mouth already?"

I smile and laugh. "Not yet, Jenny. That was just the first part of what men do. What you tasted happens before a man delivers his seed. Sometimes long before the man puts his seed into a woman."

She nods her head and looks down at my cock. Some more of the clear liquid makes its way to the tip of my cock and she wipes it from me. Jenny then goes back down and takes my cock into her mouth.

"Deeper," I plead with her. Though she has some trouble doing so, Jenny pushes my phallus deeper into her mouth.

"UTTT!!!" She pulls back. "I'm sorry, sir. So sorry."

"Do not apologize," I say to her softly. "It is natural for a woman to have trouble doing this the first time. You are so young and so inexperienced as of yet. I will help you." She nods her head and puts her mouth back on my cock. To my delight, she drops down even farther, striking the back of her throat with the tip of my manliness. She does not pull back this time, but works through the impulse to convulse. In moments, Jenny seems to have become very good at the task at hand.

Emma pulls her mouth from Michael's cock and then pulls up her dress. She removes her undergarments and then he pushes her over the table nearby. He lifts my wife's dress and exposes her white ass, his cock pulsating as he does. The man she once loved shoves his hard pole deep into her moist womb.

"Michael," she moans as she grips the edges of the table. I enjoy the way Jenny moves her lips along my shaft as her husband humps my Irish wife. His ballocks crash into her over and over again as he enjoys the inside of Emma's soft muffin.

"Fuck," I mutter as I begin to get close to releasing my seed. I want to allow my white gravy to coat the back of Jenny's throat, but then again that might cause her to vomit altogether. It would likely be much better if I have my way with her as well, if she will allow me to fuck her properly. "Stop," I tell her as I reach down and tap the side of her face.

Jenny looks up at me. "Am I doin' it wrong?" she asks.

"No, you are doing it very well. Too well, if I am to be brutally honest." We both allow a momentary laugh before I ask her, "May I see your body, Jenny? Just for today?"

Her face turns bright red as she looks away and sees her husband fucking my wife. She has never seen Michael with his rod thrusting in and out of another woman. I would guess that it is this sight that causes her to suddenly gain enough confidence to nod her head and begin to take off her clothes.

I watch for the next three or four minutes as Jenny slowly removes each garment. She is intensely embarrassed at first, but then the sight of how I react to seeing her nude body seems to have its effects on her as well. The young wife needs the same thing as her husband. Jenny needs to feel me inside her.

"Here I am," she finally says as she looks down at herself. "I realize I'm not much, but..."

"Exquisite," I say to her as I look over the young Irish woman's body. "Beyond compare." I reach out and take her hand to pull her to me. As she approaches, I put my mouth on one of her nipples and begin to gently ply my lips across it.

"James," she mutters as she puts her fingers into my hair. "Oh, James. This canna be right." Jenny closes her eyes as she enjoys what I am doing to her. Her small body shudders as I run my tongue over her hardening pink nipple. The Irish lass loves what I am doing to her as much as any lover I have enjoyed before.

"Michael...*ahhh...*" My wife's body moves along the tabletop as the man behind her thrusts in and out of her. My cock stiffens as I massage Jenny's mounds with my hands and watch Emma being taken by the other man.

"I wish I had fucked ya then," he tells my wife. "Fuck's sake, woman, yer a fine fuck!" His face is red as sweat beads along his brow. Though Michael and Emma did not have the opportunity to enjoy each other carnally when they knew each other before, it's obvious that they are catching up with whatever they might have missed. Emma soon stands up after Michael pulls his hard cock from her and takes off her clothes. Her firm breasts jiggle lightly as the man puts back her legs and pushes deep into her womb. Though she winces at first, my wife is soon enjoying each thrust of his long pole into her velvety muff.

"James," Jenny whimpers again as I lift her and carry her to a bed in another room. There, I spread her legs and go down to take a quick taste of her fine beaver. "Oh, shite," she groans as I enjoy her sweet flavor. *"Uhhhh..."* I've enjoyed Emma in this way in only the last three years. Before this time, she was constantly too afraid to allow me to do as much to her. It has become a staple of our time in the bed chamber together and I am pleased to have the opportunity to at last enjoy another woman as well. Jenny, the wife of Michael and a petite Irish woman, has such a flavorful pussy that I'm not certain that I will be able to stop feasting upon her before she climaxes.

"Fuck, James," I hear my wife say as she walks into the room with Michael. Her eyes are affixed to where I am tasting of Jenny's wetness. I smile at her and nod my head as I watch her lay back on the same bed, her dress and underclothes all gone. Her lover enters her tight cavern and begins to pump in and out of her.

"James, come here," Jenny moans. Her hands pull at the sides of my head as I move up to meet her face to face. We kiss hard and long, our tongues moving in and out of each other's mouths. My cock is hard as I consider that the young Irish woman can taste her own sweet sauce on my tongue. Her hands, small and soft, wrap delicately around my hardness as she gently caresses it.

"Ah...*AHHHH...*" Emma's petite body near Jenny moves around as she arches her back. Her soft, white skin glistens with perspiration as Michael continues to thrust his long shaft deep into her muff. *"OHHHHH..."*

"Yer tight," he tells my wife. "So fucking tight. Oh, feck, yer going to make me seed ya, Emma." His face is red and covered in sweat as he concentrates on fondling Emma's round orbs. I can tell that he is eager to pump his seed into her womb. Though he might make her pregnant, I care very little of such danger at this moment. His wife, Jenny, is all I crave at this time. It is inside her own tight cavern that I plan to enjoy myself.

I allow my cock to enter sweet Jenny's woolen muffin. She bucks a little as I push my swollen manhood into her. "James...*owww...*" Her small pussy is so tight. I'm surprised at first that she appears to have such a small hole, but then I recall that she has not had relations her husband in many months. Due to a lack of use, it has apparently tightened a little. I become even harder as I think about the fact that I am the first man she has had in so long. Pushing her legs back, I am able to get even deeper, finding the end of her womb. *"Ahhhh...fuck..."*

"I apologize," I breathe as I continue to hammer into her. Though I know that I should pull back and not be so brutal, I can't help myself. My loins burn for the final climax that I know is coming very soon. "Jenny..." My heart races as her feet sit on either of my shoulders. Reaching down with one hand, I engulf one of her small breasts and squeeze it tightly. Her body quivers with delight as she wriggles around beneath me.

"Oh, *FUCK!"* Emma suddenly bucks beneath Michael on the bed nearby. Her body tenses and undulates as he continues to force his girthy member deep into her. "Ahhh...*AHHHH!!!"*

"Nahhh..." Michael explodes inside my wife's velvety cleft, his seed launching into her welcoming, wet womb. Both lovers grapple with each other as they enjoy the intense pleasure that is occurring between the two of them. *"Emma...oh, Emma..."*

"Ohhhh..."

"Jenny." I buck hard as I begin to feel my own white gravy begin to stream from my ballocks to the tip of my hard cock. *"JENNY!"*

"Uhhhh...ohhhhhh..." The young woman beneath me suddenly opens her eyes and looks into mine as she bites her lower lip. *"JAMES! FUCK!!!"* Her mouth releases a torrent of vulgarities as we lose ourselves to each other. *"Gobshite...BOLLOCKS!"* Her soft face turns red as veins pop out along her neck. Jenny pulls at me with her hands as she moves her hips quickly in rhythm with my thrusts. *"Feck! FECKING HOORRR!"*

"Mmmmm!!!" I grit my teeth as the young wife's tight hole squeezes my cock. The entirety of this is as if we are first-time lovers. I can't help but wish for a moment that Michael and I could trade wives for a longer period of time than just this afternoon, but we cannot.

"Ay, what the hell?" I turn to see Mary Rose standing in the doorway with Tagart McNally. I'm still draining my balls into Jenny, so I don't pull out immediately as I finish humping the young wife.

"Mary?" My wife leaps up from the bed, her lover's milky sample running down her inner thighs as she does. She grabs up a sheet nearby and covers herself as Michael rolls over to hide his wet pecker.

"What is all this?" Mary Rose's eyes are wide as she looks at the situation in the bed chamber. "Honestly, this is beyond reproach, Emma. And you, Jenny?" I slowly pull out of the young woman as she is addressed by her friend. "This man is not yours."

"Please don't tell," Jenny stammers as she rolls over and tries to grasp another bed covering with which to hide her own nudity from Tagart. For his part, he turns to hide his eyes as Mary Rose looks over at him.

"You canna be doin' this," Mary Rose continues. "The law is clear..."

"Damn the law," Michael responds. "Damn the whole thing."

"And you? Will ya be standing before the Church and tellin' yer sins?" Mary Rose continues to press her friends as she stares at them. I'm uncertain as to whether I should get up and leave the room. We have yet to be formally introduced.

“Would you be so kind as to allow us to get dressed?” I ask as I stand up and allow my exposed phallus to sway from side to side. The woman at the door momentarily looks at my semi-hardness before looking at me.

“Aye, that might be best.” She turns along with her beau and leaves the doorway.

“Damn woman is unpredictable,” Michael snorts with a mischievous grin. “She saw more than she bargained for.

“We need to go, James,” my wife tells me as she reaches for her things. “Now.” I nod my head before going to pick up my clothes. Our time here is at an end.

Chapter Ten: An Irish Rose

"I'm completely embarrassed," my wife tells me as I finish packing my things in my room. Her accent has been once again adjusted to better reflect the society she has become accustomed to in Southampton.

"It was a surprising turn," I agree. "Very much so. I shall not forget it soon." There is a knock at my door and I turn to open it. There stands a boy of maybe twelve years. He hands me a folded note and holds out his hand. I reach into my pocket for a pence and hand it to him. He leaves and I read the note.

"What does it say?" Emma asks.

I shake my head. "I'm wanted at the tavern. They likely think that I owe them something, though I'm certain that I paid my bill there."

"Then go," she replies. "I'll finish this up." She takes the shirt I am holding and begins to fold it for my bag. I nod my head and leave the room before making my way out of the small boarding house toward the tavern across the street. After I arrive and walk through the doors, a young woman approaches me.

"Mr. Hutchins, this way, please." Though confused, I follow her to a door at the back of the tavern. She opens it and I walk inside to see Mary Rose. The door closes as the other woman leaves.

"Madam?" I say with some surprise as I look at the woman seated nearby.

"Please, sir, have a seat." She motions toward a chair nearby. I sit down and feel myself quiver a bit as I worry what this impromptu meeting might be about. "Yesterday," she says as she takes a nervous breath, "'Twas the first time I've seen anythin' like that." The woman, attractive and of average height, moves her long, dark hair with her fingers over her ear. Her brown eyes look at me for a moment and then away as she processes her words further. "The way you were inside her..." Mary Rose pauses and my cock hardens. It's difficult to hide such a thing from her as she struggles to say to me what she wants to say.

"Are you of a mind to report us?" I ask.

She shakes her head. "No, I'm not. But I need to know what it's like."

"What it's *like?*" I'm confused as I shake my head.

"What is it like to feel another woman inside? To put your cock into her?" Her face turns bright red as she looks hesitantly at me.

"Oh." I swallow hard as I consider the question. It is a rare thing to be asked anything like this, especially by a woman. "Well, um, I'm not certain it can be easy to describe. It must be different from one man to another."

"Did she like it? Jenny, that is?" Again, her eyes avert as I look at her.

"Well, I believe so," I reply. "She appeared to enjoy it as much as I did." After a pause, I ask, "What is vexing you, madam? Why these queries?"

Mary Rose stands to her feet. "Please stand up, sir." I do as she asks before she comes over to me. Without asking, her hands move to my trousers and she unfastens them before pushing her hands inside to feel my hard cock. "Oh, my."

"Madam," I gasp as I feel her fingers wrapping around my stalk. She pulls my cock out of my trousers as she goes to her knees. I then watch as she strokes my hardness and ask, "Why?"

She sighs. "I've never been with a man beyond this," Mary Rose answers. "I am quite the talent with my mouth." She then opens her lips and slides her mouth over my hard cock.

"Fuck," I grunt as she sucks hard on me. "Woman, holy *shite!*" Her tongue twirls over the head of my engorged phallus and I feel my ballocks draw up. "Oh, shite. Fuck. *UHHHH!!!*" I suddenly lose my seed into her soft awaiting mouth no more than a minute after she began sucking on me. *"AHHHH!!! FUCKING HELL!!! OHHHH!!!"* I try to keep my voice down, but those in the tavern on the other side of the door likely can hear me. *"Fuck...Mary Rose...fuck..."*

Mary Rose swallows my thick gravy before standing up and looking into my eyes. "Take this," she says as she pulls a folded slip of paper from the desktop nearby and hands it to me. "Tagart and I are to be wed soon. He has been given a position in London to work with his uncle and we will be moving there. This holds our new address." I open the small paper and can see that she has printed out the location of her new home in England. "Find me when you can, sir. I look forward to you providing me the same service as you have provided to Jenny." Mary Rose winks at me as she helps me fasten my trousers. She then turns and leaves me alone in the room as she exits through the door.

"What?" I shake my head as I look at the slip of paper again. Folding it back, I put it inside my vest pocket before walking unsteadily out of the tavern. There are plenty of eyes watching me as I leave. Across the street, Emma is already overseeing our things being loaded into a waiting carriage.

"Did you pay them?" she asks as she looks at me with a smile.

"I did," I answer with a lie. My mouth is absent any other words to offer her as I think about what has just transpired. Though I consider doing so, I decide against speaking to my wife about what has happened between me and Mary Rose. There is no way to completely explain what I have inside my head at this moment. We soon are in the carriage and making our way to the train station that will carry us to a ship bound for England. What I will do with the information I now have about Mary Rose, I do not know. It leaves me with much to consider.

Hotwife Pregnant

Chapter One: Shocking Revelation

Breakfast has been quiet this morning as I finish my eggs. There is something a bit off with my darling wife's mood, and I can't get past the frigidity coming from her inside the dining room. Emma is rarely so withdrawn and sullen at this time of day.

"What is the matter?" I ask her as I put down my fork. "Is there something amiss with your eggs?" Nodding my head at her plate, I wait for a response.

She sighs. "My mind is weighty this morn', James." My dear wife has yet to retire her Irish accent completely after our return from Dublin. It has been nigh on a month now and I get the intense feeling that a part of our experiences there has continued to be with her.

"On what account?" I ask. "Is it something I have done or said, my love? Please forgive me for such if this is so. There have been so many things on my mind as well since I have returned to my work at the court." Being a solicitor in Southampton has both its rewards and its downfalls. I enjoy my partnership with Phineas, my cousin, and the lighthearted conversation he so often provides. Even so, it also wrests a portion of my attention away from Emma, and I fear that this might be causing her undue harm. We did , after all, experience much while in Ireland together.

"Oh, no, James," Emma replies with a soft smile. "'Tis something else. You are a gentleman and a very kind husband." A chill runs along the length of my back as I watch her avert her blue eyes. "My dear, what is it, then?"

She purses her lips together as she considers how she will answer me. Whatever could cause her so much difficulty that Emma feels so torn in responding to me?

"I believe myself to be with child, James." The announcement causes an enormous smile to fill my face as I stand to my feet, almost knocking over my chair as I push it away.

"A child of our own? My love!"

"James." Her eyes lock onto mine and I suddenly begin to feel the same angst as she must. "You know what this means. In the last month..." Emma's voice trails off as her eyes fill with a few tears.

"No," I whisper firmly. "This cannot be, Emma. How?"

"James, you know that you are not the only one who has bedded me. Michael..."

"Michael?!" I shake my head as I begin to pace the dining room. "It cannot be, Emma. Not at all. You can tell for certain, can you not?"

"How, my love?" She shakes her head. "You must understand, I was fertile while we were with them. He put his seed inside me and now I am with child."

"But I fucked you as well." The coarseness of my language causes my wife to jolt a bit. Though we have allowed our carnal desires to envelope other people into our bed, the language of such still stings the ears of civil people during breakfast.

Emma sighs while shaking her head. "I accepted both of you into me, James. There is no way to know which of you is the true father."

"But, one of us has to be. It must be me." My heart races as I grasp for any justification in my thoughts concerning the sire of the child inside Emma's belly. "Can you not tell? Perhaps a physician might be able to tell us something?"

My wife looks hard at me. "James, you know that is impossible. All I can say right now is that there is life inside me. That is all. There is nothing else anyone can do to say for certain that this baby is yours." She swallows hard and asks, "Could you not accept this little one as your own no matter from whom it has come?"

Though I try to keep myself from showing my bitterness, I feel my face contort into an unpleasant shape. "If this is not my child..." I stop myself and gather my thoughts before continuing, "It *has* to be mine. Emma, please tell me that this baby has been fathered by my seed alone." My mind struggles to find any shred of hope that the child inside her is no one's but mine. *All mine.* Michael should not have the ability to claim anything that comes from Emma's womb to belong to him.

"He mounted me," she reminds me once again. "You saw him do as much, James. Michael released his seed into my womb. There is some chance that this is his child. But does that matter? We can love and cherish this little one as our own, can we not?" There is a brief smile that fills my wife's face as her hand moves over her still-flat stomach. "No matter what, the babe is a part of me."

"But you might not actually be *with child,* right?" I bite my lip as I ask the ridiculous question. Of course she is pregnant. Any woman would know as much at this point.

"James, you know these things. We have spoken before about women and the family way. My time has come and gone with nary a drop of blood. I have never been so late."

"But, there is hope?"

"Hope?" Emma draws back as if I have struck her across the face. I suddenly feel embarrassed to have suggested such a thing. "You wish me to be barren? Or worse yet, for this baby to die? Is that what you are saying, dear husband?" Her Irish accent becomes thicker as she grows angrier. My wife is not one to hold back once I have awakened her inner beast.

"I wish no such thing," I hastily reply. "You know me better, Emma. Please forgive such a terrible question. My tongue is sharp this morning."

"Aye, sharp and vulgar," she says immediately. Getting up from her chair, she walks to the dining room doorway. "Think better of me and my child, James. Do not wish such terribleness upon either of us." She turns and walks through the door, leaving me with one of the servants nearby who is attempting to behave as if she has not heard our conversation.

"Am I wrong?" I say to the young woman. She looks worriedly at me as if I have threatened her with a knife. "You may speak freely, Sarah. 'Tis only us in this room."

"Sir, I don't know what to say." Her face turns a light pink as she attempts to answer me. It is rare that I address our dining or kitchen staff so directly about personal matters.

"Speak plainly. Am I wrong to be so forceful in my concerns to Mrs. Hutchins? Should I have been less of a cad and more understanding?" Sarah has been in our employ for more than three years. We would have not dared to have had her in the dining room with us during our conversation had Emma or I not trusted her with whatever we said. The servants here are well paid and with good reason. A solicitor of my standing needs absolute loyalty and discretion.

"She is with child," Sarah finally says to me. "I have seen myself that she has used none of the linens for catching her blood." The young woman averts her eyes. My cock becomes a bit hard as I watch her struggle to speak of such things to me. It is considered vulgar to share such things with a man, even if that man is the woman's husband.

"What if it is someone else's? Am I to be the father to an illegitimate wretch? Do I give in to such a thing?"

"A *wretch?* Sir." Even Sarah seems to disagree with me firmly as she glares at me. "What offense would such a child have caused you? It is likely the baby is yours anyway. Surely you can allow any other thoughts to drift away?" She seems to be of like mind to Emma. This surprises me very little since the two of them spend some time together in our home.

"I suppose I will have to give some thought to the consequences of our actions," I reply while nodding my head. "If Mrs. Hutchins begins her monthly, though, I expect to be informed immediately. Can I rely upon you, Sarah? As well as your discretion?"

The servant nods her head. "Yes, sir. I will inform you of any change in Mrs. Hutchins' current condition."

"Thank you." I turn and walk toward the same doorway where Emma left the dining room minutes earlier. My heart is troubled as I consider our current situation. What will we do if this baby is not mine? Can I just love something that another man has created? Will I end up wrongfully hating my own offspring?

"Your coat, sir," Chad says as he approaches me with my long coat. "It is a bit chilly outside."

"Is it?" He nods his head and I allow him to help me with my coat. He then hands me my hat and I put it on before stepping through the door of our home. Outside, there is a carriage waiting to take me to my law practice across town. I will have twenty minutes to ponder what I have learned this morning and to consider what I will tell my cousin. Phineas is always keen to learn new things, but there are times when he becomes too interested in my personal affairs. Still, he is a true friend whenever I need to share something important with him. Perhaps telling him what has been happening between Emma and I will help to ease the burden that I now carry. Perhaps. However, it could also cause a greater level of discourse inside me as to how I will treat the baby that my dear wife now carries once it has arrived.

Chapter Two: Legal Remedies

I have avoided Phineas all morning. My cousin, though an accomplished solicitor in his own right and a devoted friend, can sometimes be difficult to speak with concerning such private matters. Emma had gone so far as to just weeks ago tell me that I should avoid speaking to my soliciting partner about our private doings. There is wisdom in such counsel, yet I find myself drawn toward sharing with my cousin. We have known each other all our lives, so it only makes sense that we are often keen to share with each other our deepest secrets.

"I can see that you have been quiet, James. Would you care to unburden yourself a little?" Phineas smiles at me as he sits down in a chair near my desk. "Did you have a difficult morning with your wife?" He chuckles, though I can see that he's serious about the inquiry.

I nod my head. "There have been strained words between the two of us this morning," I admit. "I am afraid that Emma is not very pleased with me today."

Phineas leans toward me. "Eh, the strain of a woman. 'Tis why I have kept my distance from the fairer sex." He laughs while sitting back in his chair. My cousin has made it a point over the years to remind me that he is attached to no particular woman. I think it has more to do with his fear of commitment to another than to his need to seed multiple furrows for his pleasure.

"I love my dear wife," I tell him. "Emma completes me. However, we have a terrible chasm that is spreading between us. I'm not certain I can bear to accept what has happened very recently." Shaking my head, I realize that I have likely said more than I should. Phineas will not allow me to move on at this point without giving him much greater detail as to what ails my marriage.

"Go on," he prods. "What have you done to deserve her anger?" He continues to smile, likely expecting that I will tell him that I said something improper about Emma's dress for the day or that I allowed to slip that I went with Phineas for a drink rather than taking my wife to a society affair last week.

"My wife and I," I begin as I weigh my words carefully, "Have been involved with others these last few months." I catch myself before allowing more information to simply flow from my lips.

"And?" Phineas shakes his head. "There must be more to your story, James. Tell me what it is."

After swallowing hard, I look around our office before telling him, "Emma and I have been allowing others to share our bed with us."

One eyebrow rises on my cousin's face. *"Share* your bed? What do you mean by such a statement, James?"

My body shakes as I realize that I am about to share with my soliciting partner the very thing that Emma asked me to not share with him. She is afraid that Phineas might be too vocal about our times with other consenting adults, and I completely understand her concern. He can be a bit too pressing when it comes to such things.

"We were in Ireland for a time, as I have already intimated to you, Phineas. While there, we met with Emma's old beau from some years prior as well as his wife. They seemed amenable to us, so we shared them in bed. My wife with the man and I with his wife."

Phineas blinks twice in rapid succession as if to discount what I am telling him. "Shared a bed? Sir, do you think me a fool? Would you so quickly tell a falsehood to your own soliciting partner and dearest cousin?" He chuckles. "Surely you have a better story to tell than such a terrible lie?"

I shake my head. "All is true. Every last word."

Phineas stares at me with an intensity that I have not seen previously in our years together. A dose of fear works its way up inside me as I wonder what will become of our relationship. Will my dear cousin tire of me and find another partner? Will he see me as inferior in some way and therefore a damaged side of our soliciting practice?

"Sir, there are laws," he begins while continuing to look hard at me. "Both in Ireland and in England. Laws that would see that you and your wife spend a great deal of time in the prison workhouse."

"I am acutely aware of such things," I reply. "I am sharing this with you in hopes that you will continue to honor our understanding of mutual discretion."

He nods his head. "Of course, but it is not me that you should fear, James. Were the magistrate to even hear of such things, you would be scooped up and brought before the court quickly and with little legal representation. It would be a terrible thing for one in your standing."

"One in my standing," I quip. "You know as well as I that there are those in high society who do as much or more in their own bed chambers, Phineas. Even royalty is not immune to such whims of fantasy."

"But they have the cover of those in high places," he retorts. "James, you and your Emma take such extreme risks by having such carnal relations with others. The court would deem you both as vile and reproachable. There would be widespread repercussions to you both and to your families."

"I understand," I answer. After allowing a breath, I add, "Emma is carrying a child as well. It is quite possibly of the same blood as the other man."

"A man who bedded your wife?"

"Unfortunately, I must answer yes to that question," I say quickly. "Michael is his name. As I told you previously, she had a beau in Ireland before we met and married. They were engaged at one point in their relationship, but Emma's father was not in favor of the union. Instead, she took me to wed."

"James." My partner covers his mouth with his hand momentarily as he looks at me. Phineas appears to study me as if I am some ridiculous anomaly from another time. How will he ever see me on equal footing once again after I have told him how vulgar I am?

"She is with child, and I must decide what I will do if it is not mine."

"So, you aren't even certain it is yours?" he clarifies. I shake my head. "This is indeed a grave matter, sir. A very grave matter indeed." Phineas sighs. "You should sue her for divorce and be done with her, James. It is the only way to save your personal honor."

Not believing what I have heard from my own cousin, I gasp and reply, "She's my *wife!* I won't put her out when I was in full agreement with our behavior. It would be unseemly, Phineas."

"'Tis unseemly for another man to bed one's wife," he answers. "Why would you do such a thing, man? Have you no shame?"

"Not as of when we came together," I admit. "I won't abandon her. Besides, we are both guilty of our sins."

"But she's with child," Phineas points out again. "The proof of that is all that you need, James. Enter into court and tell them that she has broken her vows. Offer nothing of your own transgressions and see this through. It is the only way forward if you wish to preserve your reputation."

"Dammit, Phineas." I growl at my cousin as I consider his words. From his point of view, it all makes perfect sense. To give up a woman who has been with me through so many things does not appear in his mind to be all that terrible. After all, he uses women as his own personal cock warmer and then thinks little of them after the fact. Phineas has no understanding of marriage or how such an institution functions.

"Consider it, my friend. I tell you this so that you will be spared the embarrassment later." He thinks for a moment before asking, "What of the other man's appearance? His stature?"

I swallow hard before answering. "He is of stocky build and red hair. I'm afraid that the baby might have characteristics that will not bear much similarity to me if it is indeed his." Fear grips me once again as I consider Michael. "Dammit, I am done for if this child belongs to him."

Phineas nods his head. "Have her separated from you, man. Do it for your own reputation. As a solicitor, you are without value if you have your wife bear another man's child. You must not allow this stain." I begin to see that my cousin is as worried about our solicitor's office as he is for my individual reputation. My actions could in fact endanger his own wages as well.

"I cannot and I will not divorce her," I tell him once again. "We were in agreement. No vows were broken because we both willingly went into this together. No party was swayed."

"And you spread your seed into another?" I nod my head. "You are a brave man, sir. If that woman is with child as well, you will find yourself in a very difficult position." I haven't thought much about Jenny as I have worried about Emma and the child she carries. As a matter of fact, I've thought incredibly little of her during the last few weeks, which is odd when considering that I enjoyed my time with her so very much while in Ireland.

"There are matters beyond our control as of now," I tell him. "Emma and I have both accepted the risks. There is much to be done in order to be ready for any baby."

"Much, indeed," Phineas answers. "You should take my advice, cousin. For your own good."

I reach out and pat him on his shoulder. "Your advice is always solid, my friend. However, I will not put Emma through a terrible divorce. To blame her as the sole offender would be ungentlemanly and completely wrong. No, we will work through this together as we have so many other things." I sigh before adding, "It was good, though, whatever the consequences."

A wry grin stretches across his face. "No regrets at all?"

"None." I can't help but smile as well. Jenny's naked body now fills my mind as I think about her and whether I might have impregnated her during our meeting. A part of me hopes that I have done so as my cock becomes stiff inside my trousers.

"There are laws, James. Mark my words and take great care in how you proceed from this point." Phineas stands to his feet and smiles at me before nodding his head. He soon goes to his desk and sits down to leave me thinking about all that has happened today.

"Emma," I say under my breath. "We are in a great deal of trouble if we are not very cautious, my love. The courts will tear us apart if they find out about our lurid time with Michael and Jenny. There is little room for understanding in an English courtroom, especially when it has to do with solicitors in good standing. No judge in his right mind would allow me to practice law if he discovers what I have been up to, and no judge would allow my wife and I to have our freedom. We risk time in prison as well as a loss of our stature in society if we can't keep quiet enough. Heaven help me, I intend to be as silent as a church mouse. I honestly do.

Chapter Three: A Message and a Meeting

"A young man is here to see you, James," Phineas says to me as I finish writing something into a case file I am looking over. After standing to my feet, I go to the front door of our office where he is holding the door open.

"Hello, sir," a lad of about sixteen says to me. "James Hutchins?"

"I am," I reply. He hands me a small note and in return I give him a pence. The messenger boy nods his head and tips his hat before turning and leaving our office doorstep.

"An interesting curiosity," Phineas remarks as he looks at the paper in my hand. "Might be of some import, cousin."

"Perhaps." I watch as my soliciting partner turns and walks away before I go to my own desk and have a seat. After opening the envelope, I tease out the letter and unfold it to read the handwritten message within.

"Greetings, sir. I am seeking a qualified solicitor to represent me in some important matters before a magistrate as soon as possible. Were you to find it in your interest to do so, I am at a boarding house on 311 Aintree Road. Ask for Mr. Scott when you arrive if it is your pleasure to do so."

The letter ends plainly enough and raises my interests greatly. Though I am not the sort to meet an as of yet unknown potential client in this way, there is little more that I have on my afternoon docket. I decide to meet this Mr. Scott within the hour.

"Phineas," I say as I look over at him. "I shall be leaving a bit early today. It seems we might have a new client in town."

"Oh?" He turns his eyes toward me. "An important one?"

I shrug my shoulders. "I'm not certain as of yet. He seems to wish some sense of anonymity. His name is Mr. Scott and he's staying at a boarding house on Aintree Road. It is there that he has summoned me."

My cousin shakes his head. "Seems a touch out of the ordinary, sir. Would you prefer that I accompany you on this visit?"

As I shake my head I chuckle. "I'll be safe, Phineas. 'Tis a nice spot in town, I do believe."

"Seems that way," he agrees before smiling at me. I reach for my long coat and put it on before stepping out into the chilly afternoon air. Winter is quickly approaching and even in Southampton things are cooler than expected, so I fasten every last button. The last thing I would want is to catch my death of the cold.

A carriage is nearby and I offer a bit of coin for a quick ride. The driver takes me straight away to Aintree Road and soon I am on the doorstep of the boarding house mentioned in the note to me. After I knock on the door, it is answered by an older woman. "Yes?"

"Good afternoon, madam. My name is James Hutchins and I am here to meet with Mr. Scott. I believe he is expecting me?"

She nods her head. "His wife is here, I believe. Come inside, please." She stands to one side and allows me to pass before closing the door behind me. The woman then turns and leads me up a flight of stairs to a room. "This is the one, Mr. Hutchins. You may show yourself out when you have finished your business here." The mistress of the house then walks back down the stairs and leaves me alone at the door. Though somewhat nervous about meeting my new client, I reach forward and knock lightly on the door of the room.

After a moment of anticipation, the door opens and a familiar face greets me from the other side. "James Hutchins! I am so glad that ya decided to come see me." The woman reaches over and takes me by the hand, pulling me into the room and closing the door before I have the opportunity to raise a question to her.

"Mary Rose," I blurt out as I look at the young Irish woman. It has been three months since I last saw her in Dublin. "Are you with Mr. Scott?"

She blushes. "The woman refused to allow me a room without a man's name," she replies. Her Irish accent is thick and lovely, exactly the way I remember it from before.

"Mr. Scott does not exist, then?" She shakes her head. My heart pounds as I narrow my gaze and stare at the young woman. "Tagart?

Your husband? Is he here?" I recall Mary Rose telling me that she and her beau were to be married soon and that they would resettle in London for work. However, I see no sign of the man in this room.

Mary Rose frowns a little as she replies, "We did not marry after all. Tagart, God bless him, was not so eager to tie himself down to me. Things did not go as planned and we have not been married."

"I see." I swallow hard as I recall our last meeting together. Mary Rose took it upon herself to give me a heavenly dose of felatio in a back room of a tavern near Dublin. It was a shocking thing to experience, though quite enjoyable. Emma, however, is not aware that such a thing took place between us.

"You are thinking about what happened, aye?" The young Irish woman grins wickedly. "It has been on my mind as well, James."

"Please," I say as I look away from her. "My wife doesn't know."

"Emma?" She laughs. "I would think that after what I witnessed the two of you doing with Michael and Jenny you wouldn't be so secretive about such things." Mary Rose's eyes, green and stunning, look hard at me as she teases her loose brown hair. "Would you like another from me?"

"Another?" Her eyes turn to my trousers and I find myself suddenly aroused by the thought. "No, I think not," I answer before my carnal self makes a fool of me. "Emma..."

"She would understand," Mary Rose insists as she interrupts. "How is she now that she's back in Southampton, then?"

I'm grateful that she has suddenly decided to change the topic of our conversation. "She is well," I reply before taking a quick breath. My face turns deep red. "Though, our previous indiscretions might have cost us."

"Aye?" Mary Rose raises an eyebrow as she studies my face. "How so?"

I purse my lips together as I consider that I have offered her too much information already. Even so, I want to have someone to talk to about what has happened with my dear wife.

"Emma is with child," I respond as my heart seems to skip a beat or two. "And it might not belong to me."

Mary Rose's face turns a little pink as she nods her head. "Michael, then?" I look at her briefly. There is no need for a direct verbal confirmation. She already knows. "Such a thing is a terrible problem."

"A very serious problem," I tell her. "If the courts were to discover such a scandal I would be ruined. This is at the very least. However, much worse could happen to both of us if rumors escape concerning the fatherage of this child." I have considered what Emma said to me just two days before. She intends to bring this little life into the world and claim by all that is holy before all men that the baby is mine. Of this I am pleased, except that it could in the end look more like its redheaded father than me. There is nary a single redhead man, woman, or child in my own family.

"You would do well to keep yer mouth shut, then." Mary Rose looks out a window nearby. "'Tis a very nice place to call home," she comments before turning her eyes back to me. "I could be of help to the both of you, James. Emma is a friend and I consider you as one just as much."

"Mary Rose," I reply almost immediately. "Would you think such a thing to be prudent? After what happened between us?"

She grins again. "You enjoyed it, aye? It could happen again, James. And again. I am not so averse to an arrangement with you and Emma."

"Emma needn't know," I reply. "Please leave her out of this."

"But, she has allowed you to enjoy other women. Have you forgotten Jenny? She certainly hasn't forgotten you or your big cock, sir." Mary Rose reaches out and takes hold of the growing bulge in the front of my trousers. I buck a little as her small hand grips me tightly. The young Irish woman knows very well the effect that she has on me. She understands the power that she wields over me, even though I would prefer to not admit to as much.

"Only Jenny," I tell her. "There have been no other women in my life beside her and my dear wife." My manhood grows within her grip as I look into her eyes.

"And me," she adds with a smirk. "At least, my mouth. You tasted wonderful, Mr. Hutchins."

"Please," I reply as I pull myself away from her. My cock is now full and ready for Mary Rose's body. Oh, how I wish that I could pierce her between her legs and fill her full of my milky creation.

"I would like to speak with Emma about what has happened between us, James. I think she would be very understanding about it all. Don't you?" She walks up to me once again. "Just let me speak to her and I can set things in motion that would make ya happy. We are friends and I know what she wants."

"This cannot happen," I say as I struggle to rid my mind of thoughts of having my way with Mary Rose. "There has been too much happen between us already."

"Still, I mean to see her." I can see by the expression on the young woman's face that she will find my wife whether I bring her to Emma or not. As far as I can tell, there are few options for me that involve keeping Mary Rose out of my life.

"You must understand that what you offer is not without risk to me and my marriage to my wife. Is there no way that you would go back to London or even to Ireland? I would gladly pay your way if you were to decide to leave tomorrow."

"I am no risk to you." Mary Rose walks up to me and puts a hand on my cheek. The warmth of it causes my cock to throb even more as I consider what it would be like to bed her right now.

"No risk?"

"None." She smiles at me. "Perhaps you could both come to dinner tonight, James? Bring Emma and you shall enjoy the wonderful skills of Mrs. Clancy at the dining room table. Her cooking is superb." Mary Rose continues to look into my eyes as she awaits a response. The fact is, I have very little choice in this matter. I can either work with her and do as she asks, or I can find myself embarrassed after the fact. There does not seem to be any better option at this point for me.

I sigh. "I will ask Emma if she would like to come."

"Wonderful." She smiles at me warmly as she pats me on the shoulder. "Emma will be so surprised to see me again, aye?"

I nod my head. "I think that is an easy assumption, certainly." Sharing my concern, I ask, "Will you tell her about what happened the last time that we saw each other?" I swallow hard as I attempt to stop myself from appearing too concerned about the prospect.

Shaking her head, she replies, "No, James. I'll leave that a secret for now." Mary Rose then pulls me to her and gives me a quick kiss on the cheek. "But if you should want more, you know where to find me, aye?" She reaches for one of my hands and places it on her full breast. Though it hides behind her dress, I can sense its softness as the young woman pushes hard into me. "I am at your service, sir. All of me. In every way possible."

After she releases me, I step back and look at her. "Thank you, but that would not be wise for either of us at this time." I reach for the door and turn the knob to open it.

"Seven this eve, aye? I will let Mrs. Clancy know of my guests. Don't be late."

"Seven." I smile impishly before letting myself out of the room and closing the door behind me. My heart is racing as I make my way down the stairs and out of the boarding house. My mind tarries through several thoughts as I consider what her presence in town means to me and to my loving wife. Though Mary Rose has promised that what happened between us will remain a secret, I have a difficult time believing her. It appears that the young woman will do whatever her carnal nature asks of her. I have seen that once in Ireland before and now in her boarding house room. For some reason, I believe that I will likely see it again.

Chapter Four: An Old Friend

Emma is quick to accept my invitation to walk with me along the shop fronts in the late afternoon. She knows nothing of the dinner offer I have accepted for us at the boarding house.

"What troubles you, husband?" she asks me as she squeezes my arm close to her body.

My face turns hot as I smile and look over at her. "There is someone in Southampton on a visit and she wants to see you tonight, my dear."

"Really? Who?" Emma seems excited at the prospect of a surprise guest.

"Mary Rose."

We stop walking as my wife shakes her head and looks up at me. "From Ireland? My friend?"

"Your friend," I confirm. "She sent me word earlier this afternoon that she is here and that she would like to have dinner with us at the boarding house where she is currently residing." My heart beats hard inside my chest as I wonder whether Emma will catch on to the thoughts that are moving through my mind. It has been difficult to get Mary Rose's sweet lips out of my thoughts, in particular the way they gently gripped my engorged manhood while back in Ireland before we returned to Southampton.

"Why would she send you word of anything? Isn't she married to Tagart now?"

"Well, she *was* going to marry him," I say to my wife, "But they decided it wasn't the best time for doing so. They are not together as man and wife at this moment." I lick my lips nervously and ache for a simpler time in our marriage, before we started bedding other people. I know that I am likely to be found out for what happened between me and my wife's friend.

Emma's expression tells of a woman who is trying to process what I'm telling her. "But why *you?* She could have easily sent word to me directly, James. Are you certain that it's Mary Rose? *My Mary Rose?*" Her eyes look sharply at me and I feel as if I am being invaded by her mind. Could she know what I am thinking just now? Have I already hung myself with what I desire from the young Irish woman in the boarding house?

"I believe I might have been easier to find," I reply nonchalantly. "Perhaps she inquired about me and upon having found out my place of business decided to send word there. At any rate, she expects us at seven this evening."

"*This* evening?" Emma grimaces. "I would have liked more time."

"Of course, my love," I say to her. "It would have been nice, but she was very insistent." I realize as the words leave my lips that I have stumbled into another morass to my story about Mary Rose.

"*Insistent?* In a note to *you?*" Emma continues to glare at me. "What are you not tellin' me, James Hutchins?" Her Irish accent becomes thick for a moment as she studies me.

"My dear," I begin after taking a long breath. "I did go to see her. I thought her to be someone else, as a matter of fact. Someone named Mr. Scott. However, she surprised me there and asked that we come to dinner." Even I am having difficulty believing what I am saying, though it's for all intents and purposes true.

"This makes too little sense." Emma takes her hand from my arm and begins to walk again. I follow along just behind her.

"I'm sorry that she chose to send me a message first, my love. I couldn't help but go when I thought it was a potential client."

"But why would she lie to you like that? Why tell you that her name is Mr. Scott and pose as a client beforehand? It makes such little sense, James. Far too little." Though Emma and I have shown no real propensity for jealousy so far while entertaining our carnal natures in bed with others, I have known that my Irish bride is very protective of our vows. In her mind, it would only be adultery if we did not both first agree upon our times with other people. She must be thinking that I went to Mary Rose to fuck her. What else would come to her?

"She had to use the name of a man in order to get the room there," I truthfully reply. "The woman at the boarding house requires men's names on the ledger. Husband's names, if the female occupant is married. Otherwise the lady of the house would not have given her a place to stay."

Emma nods her head slowly and I feel as if she might be coming around to the same understanding. "She could have come to us," my wife says. "She knows where we live. I have written to her before, James. Is Mary in some sort of trouble with the courts?" Her eyes turn to meet mine again as we stop along the side of the street.

"No trouble of which I am aware," I reply. "Mary Rose is simply staying there under the assumed name to keep the boarding house mistress placated. That is all, my love." I reach for her hand and take it into mine. "I'm sorry that she did not write to you first, Emma. Had I known that I was going to be seeing her, I would have come to get you before going there at all. Even so, she looks forward to seeing you again." I give my comment time to settle in as I think about how beautiful my wife happens to be this afternoon. I love her dearly and would do anything for her. Anything at all, even to the point of fucking someone I might not otherwise fuck without Emma's request to do so. I pride myself on sticking to our understanding, and the felatio I received from Mary Rose was not necessarily of my doing.

"I hope all has been well for her," Emma says with concern in her voice. "I would hate it if my dear friend were in trouble." She looks at me. "Is she with child?"

"With child?" I shake my head with surprise. "Why would you ask me such a thing?"

"If it has been that she is no longer with Tagart but carries his child..." Her voice trails off as she puts her hand on her own belly. "Everything seems so far out of our hands just now, eh?" My wife looks at me and grins sheepishly. "I'm sorry for my tone, husband. I think my own state of affairs is coming in on me."

I pull her close to me. "Do not worry yourself at all," I reply. "You will always have me by your side, my love. No matter what has happened with another man."

"It's not my fault, James."

"Emma, I'm quite aware of what happened and why. There is no blame for anyone in this matter."

"But, you feel that I have something to do with this and that I have been less than honest with you in some way. I can sense it in your words. You see this baby as little more than Michael's bastard child." Though I have tried to assure Emma that I am fully committed to our marriage as well as to any offspring of hers, she understands my feelings on the little one that grows within her now. We both know that there is a great likelihood that the new life inside her belly does not share my blood.

"This is probably my child," I say as I try again to reassure Emma. "Do not be concerned with anything like that for now," I tell her as I chuckle and kiss her cheek. "Your friend is in Southampton and wishes to see us for dinner. Do you intend to go with me or will I have to represent the both of us to her later this evening?"

Emma raises an eyebrow. "You would be a stupid lad for leavin' me behind, sir." We both laugh. "Yes, I will go with you. I have missed Mary Rose and would enjoy seeing her again. Hopefully all is well with her and the separation from Tagart is only temporary."

Nodding my head, I say to her, "Perhaps it is so. However, we should be understanding of her situation whatever the case. I'm sure Mary Rose has her reasons for wanting to come to England at this time, even without Tagart. I would think that the prospect of work has lured her here."

"As it has many of my kin," Emma says with a nod. "Sure, there's more opportunity in England at this time. She is probably just taking advantage of that." My wife has a way of glossing things over when she has to. In this respect, she is very much like me. The two of us have the sort of personality that allows us to compartmentalize some things that might be difficult or completely disagreeable to us. It is likely the reason that we are able to bed other people and then go away from such events with little concern about our marriage. It has little to do with our vows, but more to do with simply fucking other people.

"She has asked that we be there by seven o'clock. We can go home now and dress more appropriately before taking a carriage to the boarding house. Would that please you?"

"Aye," Emma answers with a smile. With this, we turn and begin to walk back toward our own home. There is a great deal on my mind as I smile at my wife and pat her hand as it lays upon my arm. Mary Rose could very well be planning to tell my dear wife about what happened in the back room of the tavern in Kilteel a few weeks ago. If she does, Emma will most probably be furious. After all, we have an understanding between us that we will not do such things without the other's knowledge and consent. Being that Mary Rose feasted upon my cock and then swallowed my seed, I have broken that understanding between my wife and I. There are many things that I would gladly do to keep Emma from knowing about what I have done with her friend. Unfortunately, I can't think of any at this time that are actually worthwhile and possible. No, the cards will fall tonight as they will. Fate now has me in its insidious grip. I will need to pray that Mary Rose remains quiet about what happened between us, lest Emma have her revenge upon me.

Chapter Five: A Delicate Situation

"Thank you." I smile at the mistress of the boarding house as she places a plate in front of me. She barely acknowledges the gesture as she moves quickly to leave the dining room, closing the double doors behind her.

"A fine meal," Emma says as she nods her head and looks at Mary Rose. The two women have been speaking unceasingly to each other since my wife and I arrived less than an hour ago. "You should give her our thanks and gratitude to the woman of the house."

"Aye, I'll do just that when I see her again later." Mary Rose motions toward us. "Please. Begin." I pick up my fork and knife as the two women do the same and cut into the baked cornish hen. As I place a bite into my mouth, my mind wonders about what will be the topic of our conversation this evening.

"You look well," Emma tells her friend. "I am sorry for Tagart, though. It seems that you were not the best fit for each other?"

Emma shrugs. "Not as of yet, no. But we hope to spend more time together when I return to Ireland in the spring."

"Oh? You're stayin' that long?" my wife asks, her Irish accent thickening.

"Aye. I want to see what life is like here in Southampton."

"And your finances?" Emma asks. "Do you have sufficient resources?"

Mary Rose sighs. "Tagart has offered to help me with that. He seems to be convinced that we will be together once again if we spend a short time apart. He really is a good lad, after all."

"Aye." Emma nods her head and smiles. She looks at me and then back at her friend before inquiring, "Why did ya ask my husband to see ya instead of me?" There is a sudden chill in the room, at least for me, as I quietly parse the hen's meat between my teeth. This is the moment that I have dreaded so fiercely over the last several minutes.

Mary Rose's eyes turn to look upon me. She smiles slightly as she undoubtedly begins to understand that I have not mentioned what happened between us in the tavern before Emma and I left Ireland.

"'Tis strange that James hasn't mentioned that to you." Swallowing hard, I look down at my plate.

"Mentioned what?" I can feel Emma's eyes looking toward me, though I dare not look back in her direction.

Mary Rose sighs. "I don't think it's my place to say," she replies. "James and I have a sort of bond between us since Ireland, I think. So, I asked him to come and see me directly. Of course, had he known that it was me, I am certain he woulda sent for ya first, Emma."

My wife taps my hand, which is now sitting motionless on the table. "What does she mean, husband? Tell me."

I turn my face to her and wonder how I should explain to my wife what happened between me and her friend at the little room in the tavern just weeks ago. Though I want badly to come up with something witty or at the very least believable, I begin to realize that I am caught in my own sin. I will have to be completely honest with my dear wife as to what happened between the two of us.

After clearing my throat, I respond to her. "The fact is, I met with Mary Rose in Kilteel when we were last there," I begin as I look nervously from Mary Rose to Emma. "There was a note that time as well. It was also a bit of a false precept."

"Aye, it was," Mary Rose says with a slight smile.

"And?" Emma glares at me as I struggle to completely admit my personal weakness with the fairer sex.

"And," I reply as I grip the edge of the table with my hands, "I met Mary Rose in a room at the back of the tavern where I would often have my meals."

"Kilteel Inn?" I nod in reply to Emma. "Go on." Her Irish spirit is quite obviously awakened as she leans toward me a little. My heart races so violently inside my chest that I'm convinced that it might rip through my breastbone.

"Yes. Well, we met there and Mary Rose was quite insistent about something..." My voice quakes a little and suddenly stops. How do I tell my wife that I let her friend suckle my hardness to the very end? I released into her mouth and she swallowed it gladly, a grin on her face expressing to me the enjoyment she found in doing so.

"Insistent?" Emma looks at Mary Rose. "Of what is he speaking, Mary?"

She sighs and sits back in her chair. "I swallowed his beast, my sweet. You see, I find him very nicely arranged." There is a giggle that emanates from the Irish woman as she looks at me. "James seemed very happy with my service to him."

Emma's eyes shoot back at me. *"Husband?* Tell me that she lies. Tell me that Mary Rose didna put her mouth on your cock."

I shake my head. "I'm deeply ashamed, my love. Very deeply ashamed." Bowing my head, I await the terribly fierce retribution of my angry Irish wife.

"You fucking *gamal!"* Whatever the word means, I understand the Gaelic to be less than complimentary. "Why, James? Why would ya lay with my friend?" She gets up from her seat and begins to pace though the dining room. *"Níor chóir gur phós mé tú!"*

"Now, Emma," Mary Rose says as she stands to her feet and goes to my wife. "That's no way to talk about your husband. He was too weak to refuse me. After all, you've been quick to pleasure yourself with other men, aye?"

My wife turns to look at her friend. "James has as well! He fucked Jenny, did he not? Was that so bad?" Emma shakes her head. "We have an understanding, husband. You told me it was so and I believed ya. What are you playing at, eh?" She looks at Mary Rose. "Why? Why my husband of all the other men? And *Tagart?"*

"Emma, grow up a little deary," Mary Rose retorts with a wicked chuckle. "You knew this could happen. We spoke of it before, remember?"

"What?" I look at the two women. "What the hell does that mean?"

"Inis dó."

"Éirígí suas!"

"What are the two of you saying to each other?" It has been a great frustration of mine that Emma speaks to me in Irish Gaelic when she's upset. However, to hear two women conversing about me in their native tongue brings me close to erupting. "Speak bloody fucking English."

Mary Rose turns to look at me. "It seems that yer wife isn't so inclined to share with ya just as you didn't share with her about us."

"Don't," Emma pleads with her.

"She asked me if I would be happy to bed ya, James. Before she found out that I was betrothed to Tagart, Emma wanted to let you wet yer cock inside me."

"Emma?" I look at my wife, whose face has now turned bright red. Had I known about such a conversation having taken place, I would have quickly admitted what happened between her friend and myself already.

"That was a private conversation," Emma tells her friend. "Not for his ears."

"So was what I did for him," Mary Rose laughs. "Yet here we are, letting our knickers show." She continues to laugh as she sits back down at the table. "Come. Let us continue enjoying our meal." My wife and I make our way back to our own seats.

"Then, this was something of which the two of you spoke?" I ask as I watch Emma take a drink of water.

She puts her glass down. "Aye, we did. But only just *spoke.* There was no agreement between us, husband. I didn't speak to you about any such thing, James. You had no right."

"No right?" I chuckle while shaking my head. "It seems that all the right-making lies with you alone, my love. Here you are, pregnant with a child that might be mine or might not, and you claim that I have no right. It was only oral copulation, not a true fucking between the two of us."

Emma's eyes shoot back at me. "Not a *true fuck?"* Her Irish tongue makes the comment sound much more vulgar than how I had phrased it. "You still put it in her mouth."

"I *took him* into my mouth, deary," Mary Rose chimes in. "It was very much a surprise for him, I assure ya." She continues to smile, undoubtedly enjoying the tenor of the room as we discuss such a vulgar thing. "He liked it, but what man would not, eh? I'm very good at what I do, ya know."

"And what now?" Emma asks her. "Are ya here to take him to yer bed? To fuck him more properly, Mary?"

Her friend nods her head. "Of course. I cannot lie, Emma. I want to feel yer husband's hard nob inside me. What woman wouldn't want that?" She laughs. "Besides, you wanted me to let him empty into me at one time before, Emma. You told me so when we spoke in Dublin. You want this more than he does."

"I do not!" My wife's eyes stare hard at her friend. "That was only talk between two friends. Ya have no right to him."

"Why are ya so worried? He's yer husband and not mine. Let him have his fun with me." Mary Rose's green eyes turn to look at me. "What do ya say, James? Would ya like that?"

Bumps rise along my neck and back as both women train their eyes upon me. An answer is expected, though I don't know which answer to offer. Certainly, I would enjoy burying my cock deep into the young Irish woman's moist cunt. However, my wife has shown very little willingness to me for such a thing to happen. If I were to go so far as to ask for Mary Rose to join me in my bed, I might find myself on the very sharp end of Emma's wrath. There seems to be no safe way to navigate through the morass of feelings between the two women at this moment.

"I don't know," I say carefully. "I want to make you happy, dear wife. I'm very sorry that I allowed Mary Rose to do what she did to me on that day, but I can't take it back now. What I can do is defer to you and to your good senses as to what you want me to do. If you want me to turn and stay away from Mary Rose, I will do so gladly. If you want me to be more intimate with her, I will do that only if it is upon your word. I love you, my dear. Please excuse my terrible lack of judgment from earlier." It's the best that I feel I can do for myself. Though my response is a milky muckery of bull shite, I hope that it will be enough to convince my darling wife of my love and devotion to her.

Emma shakes her head. "I don't know." Her countenance changes somewhat as she looks at Mary Rose. "You should not have done what ya did," she says again.

Her friend nods her head. "You are right, of course. I apologize if ya feel I've been too direct with James." Mary Rose smiles at my wife and the affection is returned.

"What to do, then?" Emma looks at me. "I don't know that I want this, husband. We have always followed where my preferences have taken us."

"That is correct," I respond.

"Do ya crave her?" Emma asks me.

I take a quick breath. "I would be lying to you if I said that I do not. Yes, I crave her. I want her badly, my love." Mary Rose's face turns a bright red as she looks away. This is the first that I have mentioned my desire for the other Irish woman.

Emma sits quietly for a moment, her hands folded on the table in front of her. "This is not something that I can so quickly agree to. I need some time to consider everythin'."

"Time?" Mary Rose nods her head. "I'll be here for a time, as I said before. There is plenty of time to consider whatever you have a mind to consider, Emma." She reaches over the small table and takes her friend's hand. "This would be a great time for us, though. You would enjoy seeing him with me, just as ya said ya would before."

"Perhaps." Emma looks at me. "I know ya want her, but give me my time to think, aye?"

I nod my head. "I can do that." My heart continues to beat loudly inside my chest as I think on what is being considered here. Though I have already enjoyed the softness of Mary Rose's palate, there is more to experience with her if we do have the opportunity to bed each other. Her breasts would be pleasant to caress and suckle and her sweet honeypot undoubtedly holds a world of experience for me. Her sweet essence, waiting in a wonderful bush between her legs, would be a great meal for a man such as myself. Yes, I want her. I want her so very badly.

"We can give it a few days, aye?" Mary Rose smiles at us. "For now, let us enjoy each other's company. I consider ya both my friends. Perhaps lovers eventually?" She giggles some as she picks up her fork and again begins to work on the meal on her plate. I watch as Emma does the same and marvel at how my wife's mannerisms can change so quickly over something that would have been a terrible thing in most other marriages. My feeling is that something has begun here between us. There is an unspoken understanding of sorts that will eventually need to be expressed verbally if we are to allow it to take root. Emma needs time to consider the implications of what Mary Rose has suggested and my willingness to give in to them. She has not been the instigator of this conversation, so it would only prove correct for her to take time to reflect on the meaning here. I will respect her mind on this matter. Still, I want Mary Rose just as badly as I wanted Jenny back in Kilteel.

Chapter Six: Several Concerns

The room seems a trifle cold as I watch my wife settle down on our bed. We have spoken nary a word since leaving the boarding house where we had dinner with her friend Mary Rose this evening. I have to wonder what must be going through Emma's mind at this moment.

"I know there are some things that we should discuss," I begin as I stand nearby. My skin prickles as I await her response.

Emma sighs. "I don't know what to say," she begins as she shakes her head. "What Mary Rose has suggested tonight is not what I would have expected just weeks ago. Something has changed quite a lot." My wife doesn't immediately look up at me, but continues to look off toward a dresser nearby. Is she considering packing some of her belongings and leaving me? Would she decide to go back to Dublin and to the waiting arms of her parents? Her mother would certainly be excited to know that Emma had finally left me for good.

I sit down beside her on the bed. "My dear, I should have told you the moment that I returned to fetch you to return to England. I should have never allowed what happened to go unsaid the way that I did. Can you ever find it within yourself to forgive me?"

Emma frowns a little, but then her eyes turn toward me. "I understand why you did what you did, James. I have been very adventurous with two other men and I suppose ya felt as if you were owed something in return."

"It's not that," I reply immediately. "Please never think that I feel as if I am owed. It was plainly idiotic that I allowed Mary Rose to do what she did to me. If I had been a stronger man, I would have refused her and told you about what had happened. Unfortunately, I appear to the the weaker sex in our marriage." Though it might sound that I am simply pandering to my darling wife, what I say is truly believed on my part. I allowed Mary Rose to suck on my cock and I came with delight. More striking in my mind is that there is a part of me that would allow it again, if given the opportunity. I wonder if Emma is considering that as she attempts to find what to say to me.

"Things could have been handled better," she agrees. "But ya want her. I understand as much, husband. It was shameful of me to think that I could control your cock so well as to ask ya to dip it into only one woman but not allow another a taste of it." Emma looks over at me again. "I love you, James, and I believe that ya love me in return. Let us never keep secrets between us again, aye?"

"Agreed." My wife smiles at me as she reaches for my trousers and begins to unfasten them. "Emma?"

"Quiet, James." She continues to work on my trousers until she has unfastened them enough that she can fish out my hardening pole. As Emma pulls on my cock, I groan a little.

"Emma," I whimper as she begins to run her soft hand up and down my fleshy member. "Why are you doing this?"

"Because ya need it, sir. Yer ballocks'll turn blue if we don't milk you on occasion." My wife pulls up hard on me and then leans over to allow spittle from her mouth to drip down onto the end of my shaft. I buck a little as she runs her hand over it and rubs me a little faster.

"I'll lose my blow upon your hands, my love," I say as my ballocks begin to ache. Emma understands exactly what is needed to get me to lose myself within her soft grip.

"I'm hoping for as much." She smiles at me as she puts her other hand on my cock. Both are now working up and down, causing my body to quiver as she pumps me with her closed fists. No cow could be better milked than the milking my dear wife is giving me right now.

"Holy shite," I mutter as my toes begin to point inside my shoes. My concern becomes that I will land my seed all over my trousers and the bed upon which I am sitting. Our maid is out for the evening and will not be available to clean up after us anytime soon.

"Ya want her, don't ya?" Emma asks in her thick Irish accent. "Ya want to feel Mary Rose's warm hole around yer hard cock." My wife leans toward me and kisses me on the neck, causing me to push a little of my slippery clear cock juice onto her hands.

"My love..."

"Tell me the truth, husband. Do not lie to me, aye? Would ya spill yer seed into Mary Rose's tight, wet hole?" She blows into my ear and I feel my ballocks tighten up inside my pants.

"Fuck, Emma. Fucking hell!" My body shakes as I get closer to climaxing with her hands on my shaft.

"Tell me you would fuck her, James. Say it just like that. Say that you'll fuck Mary Rose." Emma giggles a little as she nibbles at my ear. I am close to losing my white gravy into her hands as I breathe faster and faster.

"I'd fuck her hard," I say honestly. "Holy shite, I want to fuck her so hard."

"Who do ya want to fuck, James?"

"Mary Rose." I take a sudden deep breath as my seed suddenly erupts from the end of my cock. *"I'll fuck her hard!!! FUCK!!! MARY ROSE!!! FUCK!!!"* I lay back on the bed as Emma bends over and puts her mouth on my hardness, allowing each spurt to land inside her mouth. This sudden shift in strategy causes me to release even harder and I wonder whether I might pass out. *"FUCK!!! Ahhhhh...OHHHH!!!"* My buttocks tighten as my wife squeezes and sucks the last of my porridge soup into her mouth.

Emma keeps her lips wrapped tightly around the end of my shaft until I am finished popping my seed into her mouth. She then carefully pulls her lips up and away as she swallows what I have deposited onto her soft tongue. I'm in awe as I lie on the bed and watch my cock begin to shrink back down to its normal size.

"You were very loud, my love," my wife giggles as she pulls a handkerchief from her dress and dabs her mouth. It's rare to see her swallow all of my manly gravy the way that she has just done. "I wonder if Mary heard ya all the way over at her boarding house?"

"Wife," I say as I catch my breath. "Do you really want me to be with her? To bed your friend?"

Emma takes a breath as she looks at me. "Aye, I think you must do so, James. She is attractive, after all, and you have been so patient with me as I have the men that I want. Though you've had Jenny already, you are in fact a bit behind in the fucking of others, eh?" Her eyes gleam as she looks at me. "Only, I don't want ya to be fucking anyone without me there. Is that understood?" I nod my head. The shock as to what has just happened, including both the impromptu blow job and the way Emma has agreed that I can bed her friend, is still washing over me.

"Then, when should we do such a thing? Do you really think Mary Rose is intent on doing this, Emma?"

"Aye, she's intent," Emma begins. "I think Friday evening should be a fine time. I can send her a letter and see what she has to say on the matter, though."

"Friday." Just two days away, it means that I can finally feel the other woman's soft muff around my hardness. This has been the sort of thing I have craved since Mary Rose walked in on my wife and me fucking the other married couple in Ireland. To be certain, Mary Rose's eyes seemed to linger a while on my cock as it went in and out of Jenny. She liked what she saw and I enjoyed knowing that someone was watching as I lost my seed into the young lass.

"I want to watch," Emma tells me. "I want to be beside the two of ya as ya have yer way with her, James. Yer cock will be in her, husband."

"My cock will definitely be inside her." I smile as my manhood hardens a bit. "Oh, shite, I want you to watch me with her." My wife bends down to me and we kiss hard, her breath full of the scent of my seed. I can taste myself, which isn't the first time I have done so, but it's not the sort of thing I would normally do on purpose. I'm too aroused to care that some part of me is now in my mouth as our tongues move past each other.

"I want ya to breed her like a horse. On all fours while ya hold her hair in yer hand, James. Fuck her like yer the stallion and she's yer mare." She kisses me again as she moves a hand around and into her dress.

Emma begins to massage her little lady underneath as she puts her other hand on my cock again.

"Fuck, Emma." She pumps me hard as she rolls to her back and pulls her knees back. My wife aims to please herself to the point of climax. I watch, mesmerized at the way her body so quickly reacts to what she is doing to herself. Though we are married, I feel a bit naughty as I watch her enjoy fingering her furry cunt.

"I want you to put your cock in her arse, James," Emma moans. "Fuck her in the arse." My wife wriggles around on the bed as she nears completion of her devilish act. "James..."

"My love." I kiss her face as she bites her lower lip. Then, as if she has nowhere else to go, Emma begins to lose control.

"Nahhhh!!!" Her eyes close as she brings her feet close to her arse. *"AHHHH!!!"* I can smell Emma's musky aroma as her legs open wide and she continues to lose herself in the moment. *"UHHHH...FUCK!!! JAMES!!!"* Her petite body moves from side to side on the bed as my wife releases her pleasure. I cannot recall watching her please herself in such a way to completion. The act causes me to harden again and I wonder if it would be possible to blow again so soon.

I watch as my wife settles into the bed, an aura of great satisfaction settling in upon her. We don't speak at first as Emma catches her breath, but I soon ask, "Are you alright, my love? You quite nearly died, I think." We both laugh as she opens her eyes and looks at me. It's good to be able to share a jest or two with one's partner in these times.

"James, you are so filthy." We kiss again before sitting up. I can still smell Emma's essenced on her fingers.

"Then Friday it is," I say to her as I smile. "I thank you for the opportunity, but it's not necessary. You may rescind the offer if you wish."

"No, my love. You will have her and she will be glad for it. As will I." A wicked smile crosses Emma's face before she stands to her feet. She walks toward a small dressing room nearby and opens the door. "I will be getting ready for bed. Will you?"

"Yes, my love," I answer her. My wife smiles and closes the door behind her.

"Well, this has been a change," I say to myself as I smile broadly. We arrived home less than an hour ago and my thoughts then were that whatever Mary Rose wanted would likely not happen. She had given me excellent service in that tavern, but Emma appeared to be rueful of any thought of allowing her to sample me any further. Something changed, however, as evidenced by my wife's sudden climaxing with me on the bed. Perhaps she has been thinking over the possibilities just as I have. It would be correct to say that we will both benefit, after all. Our love life has been strengthened as of late due to our liberties in the bedroom with others. Emma's pregnancy might also have spurred on her decision concerning her friend. It is well known that a woman who is with child will sometimes have extreme preferences for some things sexually. This could explain why Emma has had the sudden change of heart. Maybe. We will soon find out.

Chapter Seven: A Trial Run

"Good evening, madam. Please do come in." I hear the voice of the butler as he allows Mary Rose into our home. My loins ache with anticipation as I stand beside my wife near the foyer and await her arrival.

"Mr. and Mrs. Hutchins, Mary Rose Campbell is here to see you." He stands to one side and allows the young Irish woman to walk past him before he turns and walks away. We have given him strict instructions about the need for privacy and that we would be sitting in the parlor with the doors shut tightly.

"This way, Mary Rose," Emma says to her with a smile after giving her a brief embrace. I smile at her as well, and my cheeks begin to feel as if they are on fire. After we walk into the parlor, I close the door behind us and follow the women to the sofa inside.

"Would you like anything to drink?" I ask as I watch them sit down beside each other.

"A bit of whiskey, please?" Mary Rose smiles wickedly at me as my manhood swells a little.

"Aye, the same for me, husband." Emma turns her attention back to her friend and they begin the niceties of conversation as I turn to pour the drinks from a small flask. I too will have a sampling of the dark whiskey I have imported from the United States. It's reddish color, I am told, is something special when compared to the other whiskeys found here and in Ireland.

"For you," I offer as I hold out a glass to Mary Rose.

"Thank you." She takes it and our fingers touch for just a moment. They are soft and full of life, causing my manly cock to stiffen slightly as I back away from her. Oh, how I wish they were wrapped around my shaft even now. I turn and give my wife a glass as well before retrieving another glass for myself. I take a seat nearby on a chair and sip the alcoholic beverage.

"Aye, a difference there is, eh?" Mary Rose looks over at me.

“It’s American,” I tell her. “The first time that I’ve tried it as well. I’m not certain I like it as much as the other whiskeys we have.”

“It’s not bad, really.” Emma offers a smile before taking another sip. She then puts her glass down on a table nearby and says to her friend, “So, yer wanting a good fucking from my James?” I nearly cough up the drink I have just taken from my own glass of hard liquor.

“Why, Emma Hutchins!” Mary Rose’s face turns red as she giggles. “That mouth of yers is a bit filthy.”

My wife sits back in her seat. “James and I had a sort of tussle over what you said two days ago. I just want to know one thing; why him and why behind my back?” I had supposed that the conversation about this was over, but Emma appears to want to hear something additionally from Mary Rose as well. Perhaps there is something still unfinished as far as she is concerned and she aims to see that there was understanding by all involved.

Mary Rose nods her head. “I understand that I should not have taken his cock like that in the Kilteel Inn. He didn’t flinch, though.”

“Of course he didn’t, Mary. He’s a man!” They both laugh as I feel my face become even hotter. Perhaps I should leave the parlor and allow the two of them to have a laugh on my account?

“I have apologized,” I interrupt. The two women look over at me. “It was something that I allowed because I am weakened by the fairer sex.”

Mary Rose smiles. “I am attracted to him, Emma. I know ya didn’t expect such a thing, but here we are.” She then looks at my wife’s belly. “You’ll be showing in a month or so, eh? Fancy to know whether that one’s from your husband’s ballocks or from those of Michael.”

It’s my wife’s turn to blush as she looks from me to her friend. “We don’t know yet. I doubt that we could ever tell.”

“But ya aren’t so ashamed of what ya did, are ya?” Mary Rose’s accent thickens as she converses with my wife. Though I feel a bit embarrassed by the way Emma is made to feel at this moment, there is a part of me that actually enjoys watching the two women interact.

"The baby will be ours no matter what, Mary. That much is clear." Emma's eyes turn toward me as she awaits my concurring reply.

"Yes. Ours." I get the sense that my response might be too little as my wife frowns in my direction. Of course, I will absolutely care for the child no matter which sire it happens to belong to. My cock hardens yet again as I recall Michael releasing his seed deep inside my wife's womb. He left her with more milk sauce than I have ever spouted into her warm cunt.

Mary Rose puts her glass down as well. "I want to fuck him," she tells Emma. "I know that is probably too forward, but I am not known to be bashful on these things, aye?" She giggles a little as my heart races inside my chest.

"And I can watch?" My wife has been adamant to me about such a thing. She would like to see her friend bring my seed from my ballocks. I'm inclined to be aroused by such talk as well, judging from the bulge within my trousers.

"Aye, you can watch," she agrees. "But I can't fuck him tonight."

"We didn't say..."

"I knew from the note ya sent me that ya wanted me to let him bed me tonight, but I want to do it in the boarding house. I want to know that old woman there is listening to every mutter, mumble, and moan." Mary Rose laughs. "But, I can do something for now that should hold us all over." She gets up from her place on the sofa beside Emma and walks over to me. The Irish woman then goes to her knees on the floor in front of me and unfastens the front of my trousers. "Lean back, sir."

"Lean back?" I look into her bright eyes and feel my manhood become completely solid as I do as she asks. It takes no time for Mary Rose to have my hard shaft in her hands as Emma looks on from nearby.

"He likes this," she tells my wife as she pulls up slowly on my fleshy rod. A clear bit of my essence appears at the end of my cock and Mary

Rose bends forward to lick it up with her tongue. I buck a little, my body now in complete surrender to the young woman who grips me.

"He does like it," Emma acknowledges as she gets up and comes to where her friend is kneeling on the floor. She then sits down beside her and watches as Mary Rose fondles my hardon. "Is this what you wanted, husband?"

"Holy shite." It's my only response as her friend's lips suddenly surround the head of my member before she goes down completely on me. My cock strikes the back of the woman's throat, causing her to heave a little before settling in on me.

"She seems to be very good at this." My wife puts her hand on the patch of hair above my johnson. She pushes her fingers through it as if caressing someone's head of curly hair. "Will ya empty into her mouth for us, James? I would like to know that you can at least fill her throat." A devilish smile forms on Emma's face as she watches me react to Mary Rose's every move.

"This is so delightful," I say as I move around on the chair. I had not expected to enjoy such a thing when I sat down this evening. Though it was apparent that my wife and I thought I would be bedding her friend, I had it in my own mind that there might be some sort of variance to those plans.

Mary Rose lifts up and allows my cock to drop from her mouth. "My honeypot feels even better than this, James. I cannot wait 'til ya enjoy yer cock inside me." She smiles a little before putting my hard pole back inside her soft, wet mouth.

"Fucking hell, woman," I groan as she sucks on me harder. My body quakes as I think about the servants in our home who may be listening in to what is happening just now. It's not as if I really care, but the naughtiness of it does help to arouse me even more than before.

"You'll spill into her throat soon, eh?" Emma giggles as she watches her friend enjoy her meal. "Will ya let go of yer treasure into her mouth, sir? Can ya promise me that?" My wife appears to be getting as much pleasure from watching the two of us together as I am getting from simply being suckled.

"My cock," I say as I breathe hard. I can feel my seed moving along the base of my loins toward my shaft. "I'll loose into her mouth, my love. *Fuck."* I put my hands on the back of Mary Rose's head as I feel her push my cock even further into her throat. "Oh, shite..."

"Explode inside of her, husband. Show her what load you can muster. Yer a workhorse now. Show me what ya can do, James."

"Oh, fuck. Damn cunt...*whore...BITCH!!!"* I begin to let loose a powerful volley of my seed into the young Irish woman's mouth, causing her to almost choke on it. *"Fuck! AHHHHH!!!"* My foul mouth continues to offer vulgarity after vulgarity into the air of the parlor. I'm certain that there are servants now standing just outside the doors of the parlor and listening to the sounds of their employer as he fills Mary Rose's mouth with his finest salty concoction. *"SHITE! Damned WHORE!!!"*

I grip the back of her head the entire time I am releasing into her. It is only at the end of all this that I finally release my wife's friend and allow her to sit up. Mary Rose simply dabs her reddened face with a handkerchief she pulls from her dress before patting my wilting pecker and smiling at me.

"That was a sight more than yer last time with me." Mary Rose winks at me and gets up before going back to her place on the sofa. My wife reaches over and takes hold of my soft manhood and squeezes it a little, causing a little more of my seed to express from the hole at the end of my snake.

"Was it good for ya, my love?"

"Yes, it was very good," I admit as I lean my head back and close my eyes. "I apologize for my ungodly tongue, ladies. I have no idea why I would say such things."

"A rare form of speech for you, indeed," she replies with a smile. "James, if yer mother could hear you..."

"My *mother?"* I chuckle as I look down at my wife. "Do you bring her into this conversation now?" We all laugh as I look down at where Emma's hand rests on my cock. "What now, my love? Are you going to do the same?"

She smiles wickedly. "No, dear husband. You've had yer fun for today." Emma releases my soft little man and stands to her feet before joining her friend on the sofa.

"Tomorrow evening," Mary Rose says after a brief silence. "I think we will all three be ready at that time. Eight o'clock at the boarding house."

"With the mistress of the property listening in?" I say with nervous laughter.

"If we're lucky enough," she answers with a giggle. "That old thing thinks me to have a husband and wants me to produce him to her soon. Well, I've got a lover and his wife who will let me have a little fun instead, aye? We'll have a wonderful time."

"A very wonderful time." Emma nods with a smirk on her face. "And my James will bed ya in a fine way, Mary."

"Oh, I believe that he will," her friend replies. She turns to wink at me before adding, "Will ya make me with child as well, James?"

My face turns red. "How so?"

"I'm likely fertile soon. Will ya give me a little one like Michael has given yer wife one?" My cock suddenly stiffens again at the odd question.

"James Hutchins!" Emma gives me a serious look before starting to laugh. "Ya want her belly full of ya?" She turns and looks at her friend. "Aye, then he'll do his best. I have no doubt of it, Mary. James is a stallion waiting for his mare. We've said as much to each other in private."

"Then he'll breed me tomorrow at the boarding house. I look forward to seeing what he can do." I continue to watch the two women speak about my male prowess as I pull my cock back into my trousers and fasten them back together. Some of my own seed continues to slowly trickle from the tip of my meaty beast. Yes, I'll leave what I have inside Mary Rose tomorrow evening. That is exactly what I'll do as I wet my cock inside her while my wife watches from the side of the room. I look forward to our time in bed together at the boarding house soon.

Chapter Eight: Two Mares and a Stallion

"Good evening, madam," I say to the mistress of the boarding house as she lets us in.

"Good evening," she replies. "I suppose you are here to see my tenant again?"

"We are," Emma replies kindly. The woman nods and motions toward the stairs. We make our way up and to Mary Rose's room. She is quick to open the door after we knock.

"Please, come in," she says to us as she embraces her friend and then me. There is a hint of jasmine in Mary Rose's hair as she takes hold of me as well. She has beautifully combed out her hair and it is long enough to flow past her shoulders to her middle back. The sight of it makes me throb in my trousers for her.

Emma looks around. "Are you certain we are in a good place for this, Mary?"

"Aye, 'tis fine," she laughs. "Let the old lady hear us good." The two women giggle a bit together before eyeing me. "Shouldn't ya be taking off yer clothes, then?" Mary Rose's dark blue eyes look hard at me as my manhood stiffens.

"Take off yer clothes, husband," Emma chimes in with a large smile. "Go on. Ya know ya want to do it." My wife sits down in a chair nearby as Mary Rose has a seat on the bed. My fingers, shaking with the nervousness that I feel so keenly throughout my body, manage to begin to remove my jacket and vest.

"Is he handsome?" Mary Rose grins as she looks at my wife. "Does he have a fair body to behold without his clothes?"

"Of course he does, ya silly woman!" Emma laughs as she looks at me. "Why would I let him bury his pecker inside me if he didna have a handsome body?" The two women continue to talk about me and my physical attributes as I work to disrobe. I wonder if this is commonplace amongst other ladies in Ireland? Do they conversate about their own husbands to the other wives that they know? It might not be the sort of thing that I really want to know, but I am very curious.

As I pull off my shirt, Mary Rose's eyes widen. "He's muscular, aye? A nice top, James." Her cheeks redden a little as my hands reach for my trousers. After removing them, my cock becomes erect and points at the two women. "I do believe he is interested in me, Emma. Yer husband wants me quite sorely."

Emma smiles. "He is a nice man to have in bed with ya." I harden even more as I watch Mary Rose get up from the bed. She begins to unfasten her dress and in mere minutes the dress is off of her and her petticoat comes down as well. The Irish woman is completely nude, her small pink nipples on her ample breasts looking straight at me. Though I find myself staring at the two mammaries for a time, my eyes are drawn quickly to her honeypot.

"It's..." I don't know how to address the difference in how Mary Rose's sweet cunt looks compared to my darling wife's. I have never seen one in such a state before.

"It's done in places like Paris," Mary Rose tells me.

"There's no hair," Emma says with surprise. "Dear lady, you've taken away your bush!"

"Aye, I have," she giggles. "Tagart wanted me to try it as he had heard about it from an old farmer along one of his routes. It isn't easy to find someone willing to pull them out for a lady."

"But how? It must have hurt!" My wife's eyes remain affixed upon her friend's beautiful muff. "How can ya stand it?"

"It hurt some, of course," Mary Rose answers her friend. "But only while it was being done. It feels better like this when a man has his way with me." She turns her eyes toward me. "I want you to lick it for me, James. Taste me."

"Like a horse," Emma adds. "Remember, James, yer the stud stallion." The two ladies laugh as Mary Rose turns around and bends over toward the bed. I make my way toward her as my cock drips with anticipation. After going to my knees, I allow a quick sniff of her sweet quim and ass before I press my lips hard against her softness. The woman quakes as I begin to lap at her.

"Oh, James. There. *Right there.*" She pushes into my face as I taste her bountiful muff. I have never before enjoyed my face pressed against a hairless cunt, and so I can see now why a man might prefer it over the bush. The softness of it draws me in and causes me to snuggle it against me as I taste of her wetness.

"Eat her bald beaver, sir," I hear Emma say with a wicked giggle. "Take it all in. Eat her sweet honey, James." I run my hands along her soft arse and spread each side apart so that I can enjoy more of her. My tongue slips around from her little bud to her arse hole as I eat Mary Rose. My cock strains for the warmth of her wet hole as I enjoy every moment.

"James," she moans as I lap at her nectar as it drips from her well of love. "Take me. Fuck me, please." I stand to my feet to do as I am asked and then draw my long member along her wet crack. We both jolt as the head of my manhood scrapes her swollen, erect head. I run the tip of my johnson over and over that part of her sweet anatomy as I enjoy pressing against her. Mary Rose's body quivers as I tease pushing into her soft cunt.

"Put it inside her, James," Emma pleads. She stands up and walks over to us. My wife reaches down to where my cock is poking at her friend's pleasure spot and moves it around until she finds Mary Rose's hole. "Push it in, husband." My wife keeps hold of me as I begin to slowly insert myself into the other woman's cunt. She then moves her hands to my ballocks and squeezes them as I move in and out of the woman slowly. "There ya are. Keep doing that, husband. Make sure ya empty it all into her, aye?"

Emma kisses my bare shoulder before taking her hand from my cock. She then steps back and begins to remove her dress. It appears that she is intent on having a bit of fun with us as well. I do not object as I watch my wife's breasts slowly pop out of her dress top. How am I so fortunate as to have two beautiful women with me as I thrust in and out of Mary Rose's fine cavern. Her sweet kitty is soft and warm, causing my ballocks to ache. Emma is soon on the bed beside her with her own furry muff glistening with moisture. My heart racing, I take two fingers and draw them along my wife's valley to collect some of the sweet nectar.

"James," Mary Rose moans. "Deeper. Harder. Please, sir." She moans for me as I shove my cock as far into her as I can. Finding the end of her womb, I am pleased to know that she feels my head colliding with her. "Ahhhh, James! *Ohhhh!!!*" She grits her teeth as she reaches with a hand toward her lady bit. Rubbing it, the Irish woman grinds into me and I feel my ballocks tense and prepare to empty into my lover.

"Push your fingers into me," Emma pleads. I have almost forgotten that she's here with us as most of my thoughts have gone to my other head. As I push my fingers into her soft hole, my petite wife bucks a little. She likes the feeling of two fingers inside her cunt.

"You're wet," I groan as I play with her. "So fucking wet, dear wife."

"Oh, James!" Emma grinds into my hand in very much the same fashion as her friend is grinding into my cock. I have control of both women at the moment and I am thoroughly enjoying it all. "Spill yer seed inside her, James! Be her stallion!"

I pull my fingers from Emma's kitty and lick them. True to form, she's sweet and this drives me to hump Mary Rose even harder. Taking both hands, I pull on the smaller woman's hips so that we slam into each other. My wife, seeing that I am no longer fondling her, decides to turn to her friend. What they do next both shocks and excites me.

"Kiss me, whore," Emma says to her friend. Mary Rose turns her face and the two of them kiss passionately, their tongues moving in and out of each others' mouths. Mary Rose's warm nest tightens around my cock as they attend to each other and it's all that I can do to keep myself from exploding right inside her.

"Bloody hell," I grunt as I see Emma move toward one of Mary Rose's breasts. She takes the small pink nipple into her mouth and begins to lightly suckle it. The result is instant as the second woman moans.

"Emma," she says breathlessly. "What are ya doin'?"

"Keep doing that," I tell my wife. What's happening now will benefit me as much as either woman.

"I'm going to quim," Mary Rose says to us. "I'm going to lose myself. *My pussy...*" I watch as the woman's arse tightens and I feel the familiar undulation inside her wet hole. "Oh, shite...*FUCK!!!*" The Irish woman climaxes as her body writhes in front of me. The sudden tightening of her pussy and other motion causes my shaft to stiffen harder than I have ever known it to be and I begin to spurt as well as Mary Rose continues to squeal in vulgar adulation. *"Holy fucking whore! Gobshite! GOBFUCKINGSHITE!"*

"AHHHHHH!!!" My ballocks push my seed to the end of my cock and I begin to load the young woman's womb with it. *"Uhhhh...uhhhh...ohhhhh..."* I pull hard on her hips and seat my throbbing manhood deep inside Mary Rose's pussy. *"FUCK!!! Nahhhh...UHHHH!!!"* I continue to spurt over and over again as the two women pleasure each other. My ballocks begin to ache even more before I am finished with what I am doing with my current lover. To feel her cunt wrapped tightly around my hard pole is an experience that I am so very glad to have right now.

"Oh, James. Fuck me...oh..." Mary Rose is the one who pulls herself away from me. I continue to drip with my own white spunk as she turns around and kisses my wife. Emma runs her fingers down to the other woman's bald valley and draws a bit of my draft from there. My wife then lifts it to her lips and takes a taste of it, a smile forming on her face.

"A fine vintage, husband," she giggles as she pushes her fingers into her friend's cunt. More of my white gold slips out of Mary Rose's bald muff.

"Come here," I say to Emma as I pull at her. She turns to me with surprise as I push her legs back and enter her bushy fortress. My cock, instantly hard once again, easily pierces her wetness. I thrust deep into her.

"Fuck! JAMES!!!" She grinds her teeth together as I shove her legs back. Emma's fingers slide out of Mary Rose and reach for her own pleasure spot. She begins to rub herself quickly as I hump in and out of her, my ballocks slamming into her puckered arse hole.

"You're my fucking whore!" I growl as I cause the bed to move with every thrust. There is without doubt an older woman downstairs who can hear everything that is happening in this room at this very moment. My only hope is that she does not notify the constabulary of our very unseemly actions.

"Oh...*JAMES!!!"* Emma bites her lower lip.

Mary Rose puts her hand on my wife's belly as I fuck her. She runs her fingers up to her nipple and pulls at it, causing Emma to squeal as she does. "He's going to blow inside ya, deary. Ya know that he is." Mary Rose turns and looks at me, a smile on her face, before she turns her attention back to her creamy, bare muff. "Ya might have put a pup inside me, James. I hope so." She smiles wickedly as she watches my wife continue to grind beneath me.

"Oh, fuck, James. Fucking bloody fucking hell. Oh, shite. *Focail...FOCAIL!!!"* Emma's small body shudders as Mary Rose turns and puts her mouth on her areola. *"Oh...UHHHH...ohhhhh..."* I fuck her hard as I watch my Irish bride enjoy each and every thrust of my hard cock. There have been few times that I have been so aroused by her reaction to what happens in our bed. Having her friend with us has certainly helped immensely. *"Ohhhhh...James...Mary..."*

"OHHHHH!!!" I spurt again, my seed violently exploding into Emma's pregnant belly. *"Holy motherfucking bloody pecker! Ahhhh..."* I push her legs back and thrust as deep as I can. It feels incredible to be doing what I am right now with both women. It is completely illegal as well as perfectly vile in every other respect. *"Emma, you fucking cunt!"* I finish inside her before pulling out of my wife. I've now seeded two women's waiting wombs and feel more than accomplished for doing so.

Mary Rose laughs as I collapse to the floor and sit back against the bed. "Yer only just getting started, aye?"

"What?" I look up at her as Emma laughs nearby. Surely they are acting in jest if they think that I am going to give another serving of my cream sauce to them right now. My ballocks are spent and I simply have nothing else to give.

"Thank you, husband. You have proven yourself virile once again. You've dampened my cunt after enjoying Mary's kitten." She looks at her friend. "Where did ya go to have that done? The hair removed?"

Mary Rose smiles. "We will go see someone in Southampton this next week, Emma. I'm certain there is someone who does such things. If not, I will help ya take it off."

"It is likely not legal, or at the very least would be looked down upon." I warn them. "Be careful of what you ask for in town."

"Oh, my dearest husband. Why do I have a solicitor as my husband if not to remedy my troubles, eh?" The two of them laugh as a smile crosses my face. This evening has certainly been more than I could have ever expected. With any luck, I will have the opportunity to again fuck the two of them together. That is, if my poor gents below are able to pull themselves together soon.

Chapter Nine: Damn the Consequences

"Damned rumors!" I walk into our home and straight past the butler, tossing my long coat to him without saying a word in greeting. Though rude in form, I have something of import to speak of with my wife. "Emma! Please come here!"

"Aye, husband, what's the clem?" She shakes her head as she walks toward me. For the last couple of weeks she has been attempting to once again cover her Irish accent with a more proper English vocabulary. However, her usage of slang terms has continued to persist.

"Phineas came into the office this morn' and informed me that there is an inquiry by the soliciting bar concerning moral turpitude on my part." I huff as I look for something to drink that will burn the thought of such a thing from my mind.

"Turpitude?"

"'Tis not a respectful or proper thing," I reply while filling a small glass with some whiskey. "Of all the things one could use against a gentleman of my standing. How dare they make such an accusation?"

"Who has accused you?" she asks, a concerned look on my wife's face.

"I haven't any knowledge of the scoundrels directly, but when I do find the guilty parties, I shall make them pay dearly before a magistrate. How could they say such things about me? Am I not a man of standing in Southampton?"

Emma reaches for me and puts a hand on my shoulder. "Husband, what did they say about you precisely?"

After taking a quick sip to calm my nerves, I reply, "I have been accused of seeing other women in my home. Women of ill repute. Women of the night."

"Prostitutes?" I nod my head and grimace. "Then surely not one will believe such things..."

"As well as you, my dear. We are both implicated in these charges. There are rumors spreading throughout my circle that are damning and impossible to stop. If they continue, we may both be implicated and

I cannot have that in my profession." It has been a great while since my wife has seen me so disturbed by anything. Allegations are part of my life's work, primarily because there are so many individuals who feel that solicitors are feeding upon the woes of society and using some sort of devilry to circumvent the law. "I'll sue them for their slanderous words if I must!"

Emma shakes her head as she takes my hand. "No, James, you will not. We must keep quiet for now. There's naught to be done that will not harm us even more. Keep your head high and allow this to pass." My wife, though I disagree with her at first, has our best interests in mind as she tells me that I should calm myself. She's right, after all. If I were to give credence to what is being said by attacking those who dare to attack us, it would likely mean a court appearance and some explanation of how such rumors have come about. It could mean that our enjoyment with Mary Rose would be found out and that there would be a penalty to pay both professionally and personally.

"It was a grand evening, wasn't it?" I say with a smile on my face. Emma returns the smile.

"Aye, a grand one, husband. You seemed to enjoy filling us both with your seed." Her face turns a bright shade of red. "And Mary was quite taken with you. She told me that Tagart does not have the same fire of passion within him as you. You impressed her greatly." My wife giggles and my cock grows more solid. Reaching out, I rub her belly. Emma is beginning to show a little and I continue to wonder about the paternity of the little one inside.

"It does cause me to crave you."

"The baby?"

"The thought that the baby is another man's. It causes me to desire to shove my cock into you and to spew into you, Emma. He fucked you, and I watched. His cock was deep and you were wet..." I stop as I realize the vulgarity that has begun to spring from my lips. I wish at this moment that her lover could come over right now and fuck her again for me. This time in the arse. I would love to watch it happen again.

"He rubbed me the right way," she laughs a little. "I liked feeling him inside of me, James. Did you like the way Mary Rose's tight kitten felt around your shaft?"

I nod my head. "And she was bald there. It was soft and warm against my face as I ate her sweet nectar, Emma. You should consider having your curlies plucked as well." We both laugh.

"You know that Mary Rose was unable to find someone who would see me for such a thing, James. The one she used when she arrived in Southampton was not available at the time and this is the sort of thing that is not advertised widely. The last thing we need is to have additional rumors circulating because we are seen making our way around Southampton looking for someone to remove my hairs."

"I like your hairs anyway," I answer with a smile as I continue to rub her belly. "And maybe soon I can leave a bit of me inside them."

"I would hope so." She winks at me and leans in for a kiss. We spend a while pressing our lips together and even allowing our tongues to explore each other's mouths. It's not the sort of thing that is done in polite company, and there are churches that would actively preach against such things between a man and wife even in private. However, we are safe in our own home and in the comforting arms of one another as we passionately press against each other.

We eventually part and I tell her, "I love you, my dear. I will forever be indebted to you for allowing me to be your husband."

"Aye, you will." My sweet Emma then says, "I've a party to attend with some of the ladies that I know. Please excuse me for a few hours, James." She kisses me on the cheek and turns to leave the room as I watch sway from side to side. Even her physical movements are changing because of the life growing inside her. My wife stops for a moment to turn and add, "Don't allow the accusations to bother you so, my love. They will pass." Emma then turns and leaves the room.

I watch as she leaves. "And if Mary Rose is with child?" I ask myself under my breath as I think about the woman I fucked just weeks ago. She had told me on that evening that she believed herself to be fertile ground and that in fact she could conceive with my seed inside her. Though I'm not certain that I could believe her, I feel that there is a striking chance that such a thing could happen. It has happened between Emma and Michael, after all.

"It could be yours, though," I say to myself. The baby my wife carries could be the spawn of Michael, but I fucked her as well not long after. Both of our respective jisms mixed inside her womb and the baby could be mine. However, there will likely be no way to know for certain, unless the baby is born the spitting image of the other man. Or of me. Whatever happens, I have sworn to Emma that I will raise the little one as my own. There will never be mention of the fact that an Irishman could be the child's father. I will be all he or she knows as their sire.

"Will you be needing dinner, sir?" I look up to see a house maid looking at me.

"Please let the cook know that I will be dining alone. She is at her discretion as to what she will prepare."

"Yes, sir." She bows her head slightly before turning and leaving the room. For myself, I find a chair and sit down to relax and await a meal. This evening I will think about what I shall do to avoid becoming too enraged at my critics. That will be a monumental task in and of itself, but one I must accomplish if I am to avoid making a complete fool of myself.

Chapter Ten: One More Makes Three

Emma and I sit quietly as we watch the little boy, Martin, play nearby on a quilt that has been laid out as a pad. He is sitting up now and I am growing more and more convinced that he is not the offspring of my loins.

"His eyes are much lighter than mine and he has some red in his hair," I tell my wife as I shake my head. "Michael's hair is red."

"James Hutchins," she begins as she puts down her cup of tea. "We have discussed this already. He looks more like you. His expressions are yours. There is no doubt that the lad is yours and mine." Emma smiles at me. "You fret over nothing, dear husband."

I sigh. "I cannot forget that you had him inside you, my love. Michael's seed was inside you and this child looks very much like him." I smile. "But he will be mine regardless of which father is rightfully his. I have promised you as much." My wife pats my arm and we lean close to each other as we continue to watch the young child play nearby.

"When will we find others to share again, James? I'm ready to continue exploring that side of our life."

I raise an eyebrow as I look at my wife. "You would like to once again feel another man's cock inside you?" She nods her head. "Emma, my love, this would make me very happy as well." My cock hardens and she notices as I try to move around and allow more room for its growth.

Emma reaches over and takes hold of the bulge inside my trousers. "Do you grow hard at the thought of giving me over to another bull, my dear?" She giggles and I find myself blushing. "Perhaps this time you will help him with me? Maybe at the same time?"

"The *same* time?" My face is now hot. "With another's cock inside you? Where have you gotten this idea, Emma? 'Tis vulgar."

"Aye, but only as vulgar as what we have done already, husband. I would like two cocks inside me at once." I can see that my wife is very aroused by such thoughts as she moves her hand along my manhood. My cock drips with cravings for her as I imagine what it would be like to share her cunt at the same time with another man.

"Maybe in your arse," I say with a smile. "One in your sweet honeypot and the other in your arse hole."

"James." She blushes as she now considers this. "I can't believe you are thinking such a thing."

"And you would have me put my cock beside another man's cock? Emma, it would be much better to fit myself into your arse while he fucks your blessed womb." I smile wickedly as I look over my wife. "So, when would you prefer to do this and who do you have in mind?"

"In mind?" I've caught my beautiful wife by surprise.

"Perhaps your friend Laura?"

"Laura? She isn't a man, James."

"No, she is not a man, but someone that I would enjoy bedding with you." I chuckle.

"The next one must be a gentleman of some standing, James. It's my turn to have a bit more pleasure."

I laugh. "It seemed that you and Mary Rose were enjoying each other's company well enough, my love. Perhaps another woman would make you sing as well?" This has been something we have discussed just once or twice since we joined her friend in bed. A part of my wife that I had not seen before was shown to me, and I liked it. I've been thinking about this quite often and have come to the conclusion that I would certainly enjoy seeing the same thing once again.

"Mary Rose is my friend," Emma reminds me. "I don't think I could do that with just any woman, husband. To do so was really not in my nature at all."

"Ah, but you did it anyway." I laugh again and watch as a slight smile crosses my lovely wife's face. She knows that what I have said is true. She enjoyed her time with Mary Rose as much as I. However, it would not be the wisest thing to continue doing so very often or without a means by which to defend ourselves from public scrutiny. The rumors around town at this time are tame by comparison to what might be said if someone were to discover Emma's inclination to enjoy the company of another woman in our bed.

"We will discuss this again, James. After you allow me another stud to grind into me from behind."

"Ah. Then which stud?"

She thinks for a moment. "Phineas."

"Phineas?!" I'm dumbfounded for a moment as I shake my head. "My *partner?* My *cousin?* He would never agree to such a thing and you are beyond the pale for suggesting as much, Emma. My *cousin!"*

"He's attractive and I believe that he would be a powerful man to have in bed with me, my love. Would you not at least consider him for such a thing?" Her fingers squeeze my hardness through my trousers and I tense beside my wife. She certainly has her ways of convincing me to go along with whatever she desires.

"But, Emma. He's my partner as well. If we were both implicated as participating in such things our practice would be ruined immediately. It could very well be professional suicide, my dear."

"No, it would not," she retorts. "You are both capable of keeping quiet about such things. I've seen the secrecy you share when it comes to your court cases, James. You and your cousin will join me in bed and fill me with your ballocks juice. I wish for this and this alone or you will not be seeing any agreement from me for you to fuck another missy." Her eyes focus hard on me and I can see that Emma is very serious. I will be required to somehow enlist the help of my cousin in seeding my own wife's lovely womb.

"And what if you once again have another's child? Then what? Phineas would want his child to know him."

"We shall attempt to bed each other when I am not receptive to a man's seed." She tells me. "There are ways to tell and I learned that from my own mother."

"Margaret?" I frown at the thought of that woman, though attractive in her own right, having anything to say with how we

conduct ourselves in bed with each other or those we invite. "Please don't tell me what she has told you on the matter. I might very well vomit."

"Oh, James, enough about Mother." She giggles as she leans toward me. We kiss lightly and then harder as she squeezes my cock. Then, my wife pulls away and goes to her knees on the floor and begins to unfasten my trousers to pull out my manly shaft.

I lean back in my seat as I watch my cock disappear into Emma's mouth. She suckles on me as I think about all we have done and all that we will likely do in the future together as we continue on our adventure. We have opened up an entirely new universe for us in our bedroom and I don't think that we will be going back to our old ways anytime soon. She wants Phineas inside her and the thought of it actually excites me as she plunges my willy deep into her throat. Emma's head bobs up and down as I get closer and closer to losing my wad inside her mouth. I have come to realize that whatever she wants, Emma will get. After all, it's when my wife is satisfied that I, too, become satisfied. *"Oh, fucking bloody hell...fuck...FUCK!!! AHHHHHH!!!"* My toes point hard inside my shoes as I grit my teeth together. *"EMMA!!!"* She tightens her lips around my hard pole as she swallows each volley of my white gravy. After she has finished receiving me, my wife then pulls back and smiles.

"That is for you, my love, with more to come. Now it is time for me to taste Phineas in the same way. Will you allow it or not?" Her eyes settle upon mine as she awaits my reply.

After sighing, I nod my head and answer her, "Fine, my love. I will speak with him tomorrow. We will see where he stands on such an offer."

"That is all that I could ask!" Emma stands up and kisses me upon the forehead before embracing me tightly. Though having my cousin enjoy my wife seems a foreign idea for now, I know that it will soon come true. Phineas is one who enjoys a beautiful woman in bed and I have seen him take notice of my fair Irish bride. There will be no convincing him required. My cousin will be happy to bury his cock into Emma Hutchins.

THE END

Don't miss out!

Visit the website below and you can sign up to receive emails whenever Karly Violet publishes a new book. There's no charge and no obligation.

https://books2read.com/r/B-A-GIXE-MGXIC

BOOKS 2 READ

Connecting independent readers to independent writers.

Milton Keynes UK
Ingram Content Group UK Ltd.
UKHW042246020823
426203UK00001B/74

9 798223 253570